P9-COP-009

THE SUN, THE RAIN, AND THE APPLE SEED

THE SUN, THE RAIN, AND THE APPLE SEED

A NOVEL OF JOHNNY APPLESEED'S LIFE

Lynda Durrant

Clarion Books · New York

Clarion Books
a Houghton Mifflin Company imprint
215 Park Avenue South, New York, NY 10003
Copyright © 2003 by Lynda Durrant

The story "Fox and Wolf" first appeared in *Jack and Jill* magazine.

The text was set in 12-point Italian Old Style.

www.houghtonmifflinbooks.com

Printed in U.S.A.

Library of Congress Cataloging-in-Publication Data
Durrant, Lynda, 1956-
The sun, the rain, and the apple seed : a novel of Johnny Appleseed's life /
by Lynda Durrant.
p. cm.
Summary: In the 1790s, an eccentric young man nicknamed Johnny
Appleseed feels called by God to travel through the American West planting
apple seeds that will feed the hungry and produce more seeds for planting
and trading.
ISBN 0-618-23487-X (alk. paper)
1. Appleseed, Johnny, 1774–1845—Juvenile fiction. [1. Appleseed, Johnny,
1774–1845—Fiction. 2. Frontier and pioneer life—Fiction. 3. Christian life—
Fiction. 4. Eccentrics and eccentricities—Fiction.] I. Title.
PZ7.D93428 Su 2003
[Fic]—dc21
2002010096

QUM   10 9 8 7 6 5 4 3 2 1

~

To Roger Sale,
for the work I'd gladly do for free

And to Diana, Rachel, and Allegra,
for their secret gardens

~

Contents

I

GENESIS

The Loaves and the Fishes
1782

One dark February morning in 1782, John Nathaniel Chapman was waiting for school to begin. He was seven years old and poorly clothed. It was bitterly cold in the schoolyard; older boys were throwing buckets of water into the air just to see if the water would freeze to ice on the way back down.

Like a clutch of baby rabbits, the younger children huddled together for warmth.

A neighbor boy grabbed Johnny by the elbow and spun him away from the clutch. Johnny tripped over a frozen clod of earth and fell hard. The neighbor boy shouted, "My pa says yer pa was throwed out of the army for bein' a drunk!"

Another boy jeered, "Yeah, General George Washington himself kicked him out."

The older boys stopped tossing water and stared.

Johnny's older sister, Elizabeth, knelt beside him

and said, "Don't listen to them. They don't know anything."

But Johnny knew already what they meant, or at least he thought he did. It had something to do with Pa being in bed all the time. It had something to do with being so poor, and the whispers of the townspeople wherever he went.

An older boy gave a water bucket a mighty heave. Shards of ice fell onto the frozen ground of the schoolyard and broke around Johnny's ears like shattering glass.

🌲🌲🌲

"Pa," Johnny said as they sat in front of the hearth fire that evening, "why'd you come home from the war so early, when there was plenty of war left to fight?"

His father turned away from the fire, his face in shadow. "I'd had enough of killing."

"Were you worried about Elizabeth and me? Is that why you came home?"

"Johnny," his stepmother said from her seat at the spinning wheel. "Your father used to be a Massachusetts minuteman. He fell in with Colonel John Wetcomb's regiment at Lexington and Concord on April nineteenth, 1775.

"Your father fought in the Revolution until 1780," she continued. "I needed him on the farm after that. You can be proud of your father."

My pa says yer pa was throwed out of the army for bein' a drunk.

Johnny spoke up. "Is that true, Pa?"

Nathaniel Chapman stumbled to his feet. "I'm going to bed." He never said another word about the war. Not to Johnny. Not to anybody.

🌳🌳🌳

Johnny had been born in Leominster, Massachusetts, on September 26, 1774, and was baptized in the Leominster Congregational Church soon after. According to legend, the apple trees were in blossom the day he was born. Of course, that isn't true.

It is true that his mother "went home" giving birth to his brother Nathaniel. Nathaniel went home a week later. Johnny was two. His big sister, Elizabeth, was four. They needed a mother, and their father needed a wife: Nathaniel Chapman married Lucy Cooley. She was a good woman, Johnny thought: patient, kind, and strong. Johnny grew up in Longmeadow, Massachusetts, on the eastern bank of the Connecticut River, with sister Elizabeth and ten half brothers and sisters. Fourteen people in the smallest log cabin in town! Mostly, he lived outside.

A neighbor gave the Chapmans some apple seeds when Johnny was nine. His father planted the seeds in holes as deep as a man's hand is wide and five strides apart, three apple seeds in each.

"Why three apple seeds in a hole, Pa?" Johnny asked. "Why not just the one?"

"There's a little poem about it, Johnny," his father replied. "Passed down by orchard men through the ages.

> "One for doubt under the hoe,
>   One to sprout, and one to grow."

His father gave him a handful of seeds. "Here, you try it, three apple seeds per hole."

Johnny carefully counted out three apple seeds each time his father had a hole ready for sowing. The poem satisfied him like no other words he'd ever heard. It meant someone had reckoned it out, after who knows how many trials and errors and hungry winters. An orchard man in ancient days had discovered just how many apple seeds should be sown in each hole to guarantee a tree. And without wasting any precious seeds. Even better, this orchard man had passed his hard-won wisdom along to his neighbors, so future generations could reap apples just as he once had.

Johnny gazed in wonder at the mounds of earth. He could just picture the apple seeds snug within. All those apples as yet uneaten, as summer after summer ripened into autumns as yet unseen!

This miracle seemed to him as close to a guarantee as one could hope for in this life.

Seven years later, his trees bore fruit.

Johnny spent his sixteenth spring and summer in

6

the middle of the Chapmans' orchard. He gaped in astonishment as the apple branches turned bright red in April, blossomed in May, leafed out in June, rested in July, and bore fruit in late August, September, and October.

Wasn't it astounding that the New World had no native apple trees? Every orchard had to be planted by the hand of man and not by God.

Just like everyone else in Longmeadow, Johnny went to church every Sunday morning. Every Sunday afternoon, Johnny would leave the meetinghouse scratching his head and pondering the apples on the forbidden Tree of Life, Adam and Eve's punishment, the Fall of Man, the New World's stupendous bounty but without the blessing of the apple. Whenever he tried to reason it out, his brain would get as muddled as a corn-and-cranberry pudding.

According to Pastor Isby, "a flaming sword turned every which way," guarding forevermore the road to the Tree of Life. Adam and Eve were exiled, driven to the east of Eden. But as Johnny saw it, there were apples east of Eden, too! Had to be, if folks were eating them now. The apple was perfection, curse, and mercy.

In late summer, the first of the apples were ripe for picking. Just as the butcher uses every part of the pig but the squeal, Johnny's stepmother used every part of the apple but the stem. She was a handy cook:

applesauce, apple pies, scalloped apples with cinnamon, apple pan dowdy, apple dumplings, apple–black walnut cake, apple crisp, apple-rhubarb-cranberry compote, apple chutney with mint, dried apples, apple cobbler, and apple butter. There were always plenty of apples to be eaten out of hand after school.

For the first time ever, no one in the Chapman family went to bed hungry. And for the first time ever, the Chapman family could offer charity to their neighbors, in the form of apples. There were plenty more moss-wrapped apples in the root cellar as well—better than money in the bank.

Johnny saved the seeds and planted again the next spring.

His family's abiding hunger, satisfied for once, was a powerful blessing, for it was this hunger that first gave him the notion of the neighbor, the apple seed, and his own version of the loaves and the fishes.

It was a parable from the Bible: The Teacher blessed seven loaves of bread and a few small fish, and thus fed four thousand people who had been in the desert, without food, for three days. "And they did all eat, and were filled: and they took up of the broken meat that was left seven baskets full."

It was those seven baskets full of broken pieces that held Johnny's wonder and attention. What those four thousand people had left over was more than they had to begin with! The more bread they shared, the more bread remained! How could that be? It was a miracle by all accounts and witnesses.

But to Johnny, these were baskets full of Massachusetts apples, not Galilee bread. The apple was its own miracle, if people would only pay attention.

Eat one apple and plant three apple seeds. In seven years, you'll have enough apples to feed your family through an entire winter.

Plant three more apple seeds. In seven years, you'll have enough apples to give a neighbor, to feed his family through an entire winter.

Plant three more apple seeds, and give another neighbor enough apples to feed him and his family through the winter.

Now imagine a thousand neighbors, imagine four thousand neighbors, every last one of them eating apples and planting apple seeds to help even more folks through the winter.

Were this to happen, there'd be no reason for anyone on this earth to be hungry again. Ever. Seven years for seven baskets full of trust, bounty, and patience paid back four-thousand-fold.

All this miracle needed was the sun, the rain, and the apple seed—the sun and the rain warmed and watered the earth, the flocks and fruits increased in the fullness thereof. Just like the loaves and the fishes, the more apples you shared, the more apples you would have to share.

If you give away everything you have, you have more, not less.

Johnny dreamed of an endless parade of apples, more than even the hungriest boy could ever eat. The Newtown Pippin was best for cider, the Northern Spy for baking. His family's Boston Belles were by far the prettiest. The most adaptable was the McIntosh. Johnny's personal favorite was the Rambo, which would store in a root cellar fresh as a daisy all the way through May.

Once chores and school were done with, he'd kick off his shoes, regardless of the weather, and wander in the woods near Longmeadow. Johnny liked people well enough, but there within the woods, the trees and animals seemed to hold him in a welcoming embrace.

In the spring, the does would come right up to him to show off their fawns. The first time he stroked a fawn's withers, its heart pattered fast as a hummingbird's wings. After a visit or two, both Johnny and the fawn calmed themselves soon enough.

The squirrels, the chipmunks, the deer families, the raccoons and woodchucks, and the birds followed him as though he were the Pied Piper of Hamelin.

He always had food for the animals (never the seven baskets full—the Chapmans were too poor—but he might scatter seven handfuls of cornmeal on a good day).

Deep within those Massachusetts woods he'd think: *My childhood is coming to an end, and a man needs an occupation. What sort of occupation can I have? How can I combine my love of the woods with the miracle of the apple?*

He knew, just as certainly as the wintering earth waits patiently for spring, that God would give him his answer someday.

His schoolmaster had told him of the cathedrals in England, France, and Spain. These were churches the size of a farmer's fifteen-acre cornfield, with ceilings soaring to the height of the tallest black walnut tree. A man might spend his entire life building one wall of such a church, cutting the stone and chinking it in place. He might pass the occupation along to his sons, who in turn would pass the work along to their sons.

Johnny was sure those cathedrals were mighty grand. But what could be grander than a Massachusetts black walnut tree, soaring so high that no one but God Himself could see the treetop? A black walnut tree is the last tree in the forest to leaf out: It's mid-June before its branches are covered. It's the first to lose leaves, too: In early September, they're already turning red and falling to the ground.

Black walnut trees grow the slowest, but that makes their wood the strongest. A board cut from black walnut will hold fifteen times its weight, easy. Just like the men who built those churches in the Old World, Johnny reckoned, a man could spend his entire life watching a black walnut tree grow, then pass the occupation along to his sons, who in turn would pass the work along to their sons. It seemed to him a fine and honorable way to make a living.

At twenty, he tried to explain this to his half sister Persis. "Watching the black walnut trees grow could be a family business, sister, just like the generations who built the cathedrals of old."

"Johnny." His fifteen-year-old sister looked away sadly. "Either you're tetched in the head or you're tetched by God, and I don't know if there's a difference."

"Perhaps I'm like the black walnut tree—by that I mean growing the slowest, and at the same time growing the strongest. God will reveal my occupation to me. He will give me the answer I seek. I just have to be patient."

"I hope so, Johnny."

The Chapmans all looked alike: Hair as thick and brown as an otter's pelt in midwinter. Tall and gangly, with limbs sapling thin and strong. And just like saplings, they'd learned to bend in the wind.

It was the regimental parades that finally drove Johnny out of Massachusetts. When he was a boy, his father took to making applejack from the town's windfall apples. Now Nathaniel used the family's windfalls to make even more. On parade days, the boys of Long-meadow would cast their stones: "Yer pa's yeller. Yer pa's lazy. Yer pa's a drunk."

Johnny and his brothers and sisters had long since inured themselves to the jeers of the town's boys. And yet, for as long as he could remember, Johnny had been ashamed of his father.

And ashamed of being ashamed.

On parade days, Nathaniel Chapman wasn't allowed to march. He wasn't allowed to wear his army uniform. The mayor did not call out his name, although it was on the regimental honor roll for the town.

There was one blessing, praise His name. The bar-keep at the Fox & Rogue would not stand Nathaniel Chapman a free ale, as was his custom for the other vet-erans of Longmeadow.

Johnny's father had deserted from the army, had walked away from the cause of Liberty, when other men had remained and died for it. He would hide in the house on parade days and drink applejack. By the time Johnny was twenty-two, his father would hide in the house all day and drink applejack if it wasn't a parade day, too.

Nathaniel Chapman's very soul stank of applejack.

By then, Johnny was learning the trade of lumber-man. As the sun set behind Longmeadow, the western wilderness would glow as though on fire, just like the flaming sword turning every which way, guarding the road to the Tree of Life.

The Chapmans had an abundant orchard now; Johnny's family need never go hungry again.

It was during one of those fiery sunsets that he decided to try his own hand in the wilderness, to take his own bite out of the apple.

THE FIRST CIRCLE
1797~99

In 1797, when he was twenty-three, Johnny walked to Pittsburgh, Pennsylvania.

Westering pioneers were paying good money for flatboats (also known as broadhorns), to give them ready access to settlements down the Ohio River and to the borderlands. Johnny was right handy with a saw and hammer.

🌳🌳🌳

In late December 1798, it had rained like fury for weeks. The streets were as muddy as the Ohio, Allegheny, and Monongahela River bottoms combined. The men of Pittsburgh were in a foul and sullen mood and eager to drown their sorrows. The barkeeps were just as eager to oblige them.

It was in that same week that Mr. Thomas Wells, a sojourning gentleman from Rochester, New York, arrived in Pittsburgh. It was his intention to round out his memoirs with agreeably pungent anecdotes about the American West. Mr. Wells rented the room above the Badger's Egg Tavern and strolled down Main Street, taking in the citizenry.

He lasted two days.

"There are only four churches in Pittsburgh, and six times as many taverns and public houses, all of them live," he shouted to the barkeep. His bitter yet accurate comment was the talk of Pittsburgh, at least for a few days.

It was a fair assessment—but Johnny's own impression of Pittsburgh echoed Judges 17:6: "In those days there was no king in Israel, but every man did that which was right in his own eyes." That was Pittsburgh, all right.

Those twenty-four taverns served spirits and applejack round the clock to the two thousand souls who called Pittsburgh home. Mostly, those souls were lumbermen and carpenters just like Johnny.

Because of his father, Johnny had made a vow that he would never drink spirits or applejack. He drank from a spring that flowed into the Monongahela River. He did have to eat in the taverns, though.

There was a lumberman by the name of Phineas Filo, a giant of a man. He was about the size of the trees he cut down and as prickly as a porcupine, on account of his peculiar name.

It was the early winter of 1798–99 when Phineas burst into the Skunk & Opossum Tavern, spoiling for blood.

"Where's the Dutchman?" he roared. *"Where's the Dutchman?"*

Johnny knew what was coming; he picked up his plate and shrank into a corner.

Apparently, the Dutchman was not among those present at the Skunk & Opossum. But the lumbermen taking their leisure at the tables sprang to their feet and spilled out onto Main Street. Some were eager to defend the Dutchman's honor, others saw the argument Phineas's way. Still others ran from public house to public house, either looking for the Dutchman or calling the alarm for others to do the same.

In the blink of an eye, the taverns were empty and all of Pittsburgh was brawling in the street.

The only law was the American regiment quartered at Fort Pitt. Johnny took it upon himself to run up the hill to the fort.

"Good gentlemen!" he shouted, pounding at the sally port. "Open your gates. I come from the town!"

The sally port opened a trickle. A soldier stuck his nose out. "State your business."

It had always been Johnny's custom to explain the world and her signs and wonders with Bible verses. He could spout verses the way a spring purls water—in a constant, steady stream.

"Your business?" the soldier barked.

Johnny was breathing hard. He gasped, "'Why do the heathen rage, and the people imagine a vain thing?'"

The soldier scowled. "Those lumbermen at it again?"

The sally port slammed shut. In a moment or two a company of soldiers sallied forth and marched double time down the hill. Johnny followed. The soldiers broke ranks once they were upon the scrapping lumbermen. A mighty roar rose up from the town.

"'Let judgement run down as water, and righteousness as a mighty stream!'" Johnny shouted.

More soldiers poured forth to join their countrymen in battle. They almost knocked him down.

🌳🌳🌳

Johnny worked for Mr. Joshua Stadden in his Pittsburgh lumberyard and flatboat dockyards. His first job was to make pegs from the heartwood of oak trees, a tree's heartwood being the strongest. After a few months, he was allowed to pound these oaken pegs into the broadhorns' keels and decks and into the under frame.

Mr. Stadden taught Johnny to use oaken pegs, not iron nails. Nails won't expand and contract in consort with wet and dry wood the way heartwood pegs will.

Mr. Stadden warned him not to stint on the pegs. Johnny drilled the holes, then pounded pegs, one pair per six inches of keel board or floorboard. Johnny worked as hard as the day is long.

Mr. Stadden told him, "Mr. Chapman, my broadhorns cost more than the competition, but you do get what you pay for in this life."

"Yes, sir."

"All too often," Mr. Stadden continued, "pioneers buy the cheapest broadhorn on offer. Usually at Mr. Tubman's dockyards. Mr. Tubman's broadhorns catch the currents down the Ohio, break apart, and sink, faster than a cornpone in a bowl of milk.

"Then the pioneers and all their floatable worldly goods—tea chests, barrels, shoes, sealed jars of apple butter—will lay up on the Virginia shore near Wheeling, or on the Ohio shore near Marietta."

Mr. Stadden drilled a hard stare into Johnny. "That is, if they're lucky. If not, the pioneers will wash up farther down on the Indiana shore near the Whitewater River, where Mr. Tubman and the Shawnee will send them to their reward. Do you understand, Mr. Chapman?"

Johnny gulped. "Two pegs per six inches of keelboard. Yes, sir."

🌳🌳🌳

For some folks, life is like that story of the frog that jumped into a slowly cooking pot of stew. The frog became hotter and hotter as the stew cooked, but he hardly noticed the difference, the change was so gradual.

For Johnny, October 15, 1799, was like a sudden lapful of scalding tea. His life changed forever.

The lumbermen at Mr. Stadden's were working especially hard to finish this year's broadhorns before the winter snow flew. The hot weather and hard work put them in mind of cider.

"Mr. Chapman," Mr. Stadden said one morning at dawn's first light, "you're the only honest hand I've got. Would you oblige me by heading south to the town of Elizabeth? Mr. Van Kirk has his cider press there. These thirsty men have worked determinedly all summer, and they deserve a treat. It is the season for cider, and we may get a good price. Just follow the river and buy two good-sized casks."

Mr. Stadden gave him the coinage, some rope, and the use of his horse, Clabber, for the twenty-mile journey. Johnny followed the Monongahela River south, up the river path.

The trip to Elizabeth filled his heart with gladness and his voice with praise, what with the chance to ride a horse again and take in the mid-October color. The oaks, sumacs, hemlocks, ashes, and buckeyes were in pied shades of yellow, orange, red, and plum, as bright as jewels in a pirate's treasure chest.

Johnny came to a grove of maples and dismounted. Clabber and he needed to drink. The falling maple leaves, as dark red as the skin of a Rome apple, pattered softly onto the clear water. Within the rock pools, minnows swam.

Amid the fiery palette were birds, thousands of them, all calling to each other by kind. The red-winged blackbirds settled in the yellow sycamores clinging to the riverbank. The golden finches were in a patch of flaming-orange shagbark hickories. Within the red oaks, bright-green Carolina parakeets took their ease.

After a moment of quiet, the flocks burst forth from the trees, winging their way south for the winter.

"Clabber, look! The Lord's beautiful dwelling place! 'How amiable are thy tabernacles!'" Johnny shouted. The horse snorted and widened his eyes in alarm.

Amiable, and yet there was something missing, something Johnny couldn't quite put his finger on.

Elizabeth, Pennsylvania, was a quiet village, on even land nestled within a wide bend of the Monongahela River. Johnny came upon it suddenly. Just as suddenly, he knew what was missing from these Pennsylvania woods.

For all around Elizabeth were orchards, entire fields given over to the growing of fruit trees. Smooth-barked cherry trees reflected the evening sunlight. Apple and peach trees stretched in orderly rows to the horizon and beyond. The trees were so laden with fruit that the Elizabeth orchard men had been obliged to prop up the branches with forked sticks.

Fruit trees lose their foliage late; the lower branches were green still. Autumn color surmounted the top branches and rolled downward, spilling through the tree rows like a wave.

The very air was scented with apples. All Johnny and Clabber had to do was follow their noses to Mr. Van Kirk's cider press.

Riverside, the press was an immense contraption on stilts. Men poured apples by the barrelful into a vat the size of a one-room cabin. A great circle of oaken boards was placed on the apples, then levered downward into the press. The apple juice gushed forth into other oaken vats. The women of the town poured out the cider into casks to be sold or stored for later.

"Good day, sir," a man called out to Johnny. This man was almost as big around as the apple barrels he worked with. He was nearly bald. His red beard and mustache grew around his face like licks of flame.

"I'm William Van Kirk. How may I help you?"

Johnny said, "I've come from Pittsburgh to buy cider for the workingmen there."

"Pittsburgh is no place for the likes of you, sir. Stay here and help with the cider pressing. I'm paying good wages. I need all the hands I can get."

"Thank you for your kind offer, but my employer waits for cider just 'as the hart panteth after the water brooks.'"

Mr. Van Kirk gave Johnny a cool look. "A preacher, are you?"

"No, sir, and yet everywhere I go, I bring news fresh from Heaven."

"Is that right?"

Some of the early cider was already fermenting. As a breeze sailed upriver, the strong scent of applejack brought tears to Johnny's eyes and a sob to his throat.

My father! A good man broken by a town that could not forgive his cowardice! A man who tried to console himself with applejack, only to shatter his own worth all the more.

"Is there something wrong, sir?" Mr. Van Kirk asked.

With his sleeve, Johnny wiped the tears away from his cheeks.

"John Chapman's my name," he replied. "Your fair town puts me in mind of home. My father back in Massachusetts was a patient orchard man. He was partial to the apple called the Boston Belle."

"The Boston Belle doesn't grow in these parts, Mr. Chapman. Our winters aren't harsh enough," the other man answered. "But try this one."

Mr. Van Kirk held out an apple with a blush of good red color and yellow-green speckling from stem to stern. Johnny was powerfully hungry, what with all the riding since dawn. He bit into an apple with crunchy white flesh. The abundant juice ran down his chin.

"Delicious. The variety?"

"That's a McIntosh," Mr. Van Kirk replied proudly. "We're making cider from McIntosh apples today."

Clabber nudged Johnny's shoulder. He took another mighty bite, then gave the horse the rest.

Mr. Van Kirk frowned. "That apple was for you, sir."

Johnny had to chew for a bit before replying. Clabber chewed his share as well, his eyes bright, nodding his head in time with his jaws. The horse nudged Johnny again, so hard he almost fell over.

"And I thank you for it, Mr. Van Kirk," Johnny replied at last. "Clabber here has worked harder than I have today, and 'God loveth a cheerful giver.'"

Mr. Van Kirk gave him another cool stare. Finally, his face broke into a smile. "Have another apple, Mr. Chapman."

"Thank you."

It was at that moment that the crew tipped over the vat. A great sluice of apple pulp and seeds ran out onto the ground. They shoveled this pomace into the Monongahela. The river, already full of pomace, bubbled and popped sluggishly. Bright-brown apple seeds sank to the bottom without a trace.

"You're throwing away the apple seeds?"

"Sad to say we've no use for them here, Mr. Chapman. We lack the open space to grow more nursery trees. A shame, for these hungry pioneers appreciate every apple they can find."

Thunder and lightning! Johnny fell to the earth, trembling. Finally, the Spirit of the Lord had shown him the way!

The westering pioneers! The apple seeds! My love of the woods! The loaves and the fishes! My true occupation at last!

On his knees, he spread out his arms and shouted, "I shall gather apple seeds and plant them in the borderlands on behalf of the pioneer folk! Thank you! O Lord, thank you for revealing my life's mission to me!"

Mr. Van Kirk had stepped back, as did the orchard men and Clabber.

"I beseech you, good sir, don't throw away the apple seeds," Johnny cried out. "For in those seeds is the very meat and drink of this nation! 'Sing unto the Lord a new song; for he hath done marvellous things!'"

"You've got no cause to kneel," Mr. Van Kirk said in a shaking voice. "Take as many apple seeds as you like."

Johnny jumped to his feet and prepared to dive into the river for the precious seeds. Just in time, Mr. Van Kirk and his crew held him back.

"Wait for tomorrow's sluice, Mr. Chapman," Mr. Van Kirk ordered. "They'll be plenty of apple seeds then."

🌳🌳🌳

As he waited for supper, Johnny studied Mrs. Elizabeth Van Kirk. She was a wonder. Her hair was the same warm brown as a female cardinal's feathers. Small and slight, she'd trod a circle right into the cabin's dirt floor with her endless rounds from hearth fire to table to dish basin to hearth fire to table to dish basin. . . .

Her forearms were the size of a man's from working so hard.

She served an excellent supper. Johnny, the orchard men, Mr. Van Kirk, and the Van Kirks' son, Willie, who was fifteen, ate cheese and fresh apple pies with crusts so substantial, they could eat the wedges out of hand. They all drank quarts of new milk.

The Van Kirks had pear and quince trees in their front yard. They ate pear and quince cobblers, too.

The crew slept in the attic. Clabber and Johnny slept in the barn. He was weary yet couldn't sleep, so inspirited was he to begin his life's work. The hay crackled all night as he tossed and turned.

At breakfast the next day, Mrs. Van Kirk served great bowls of baked apples with plenty of toasted oatmeal and maple syrup. There were jugs of cream to pour over the top.

Johnny bought the two casks of cider from Mr. Van Kirk and lent a hand with the cider making until the nooning.

After more milk, cheese, and apple pies, Mrs. Van

Kirk helped him wash the apple seeds out of the pomace. Willie gave Johnny a pair of leather pouches with shoulder straps and packed the apple seeds inside.

While they worked, Johnny spoke of nothing but his newfound calling. "My mission," he kept repeating, "is so simple! I'm to plant orchards in the wilderness. My life's true mission at last."

"It's a dangerous mission you're setting out on, Mr. Chapman, what with the bears, the cougars, and the Indians," Mrs. Van Kirk said.

"I think it sounds exciting!" Willie exclaimed.

"No, you don't." Mrs. Van Kirk frowned at him.

"'Blessed are the meek,' Mrs. Van Kirk, for I have never had an enemy in this life," said Johnny.

It was Mrs. Van Kirk's turn to stare. She then rose and went into the next room. She returned with a Bible big enough to be held in both her hands. "This is for you, Mr. Chapman."

"I cannot take your Bible!"

"I have another. Please, Mr. Chapman, take it. I ask only that you come back here after the apple seeds are planted and bring me news of my sister. Her name is Esther, and she's married to Mr. James Bushnell of Champaign County, Ohio."

She pushed the Bible into his hands. The thick leather cover was the same dark brown as his apple seed pouches.

"I'll plant a good portion of these seeds round her

property," said Johnny. "As she watches the trees grow and eats the apples, she'll think of you. Thank you for the Bible."

"Mr. Chapman, are you aware that apple trees bear more fruit if they grow accompanied by another variety? These are McIntosh apple seeds. You'll need another strain."

"I didn't know that."

"I want to give you something else."

Mrs. Van Kirk went into the side room. She soon returned with a small sack of apple seeds.

"These are Ashram's Kernel seeds, Mr. Chapman. From Turkey; the finest apple I know for eating out of hand. Plant the Ashram's Kernel and the McIntosh apple seeds together in your wilderness orchards and both strains will be the stronger, and the sweeter, for it."

"I'll do that. And thank you."

3

STARTING OUT
1799

Mr. Stadden sat in his rocking chair and wrung his hands in dismay. "Mr. Chapman, I beg you to stay in Pittsburgh! You're the best keelman and deckman I've got. And the winter is coming on! You'll not survive the four months of winter, alone in the wilderness."

Johnny stood resolutely in front of the hearth fire. "God will provide, Mr. Stadden, just as He has so far."

"Have you a rifle?"

"I don't need one. I haven't an enemy in this world."

"How will you hunt game for food?" Mr. Stadden asked in alarm. "How will you protect yourself against the panthers? The bears? The wild boar and rattle-snakes?"

"I've given this considerable thought," Johnny said slowly. "I've decided I will eat no food that doesn't come from the soil. Nor will I kill the animals of the forest for any reason. I'm going into their home to plant these apple seeds, if they'll have me. It seems to me that's interference enough."

Mr. Stadden stood up abruptly. "Mr. Chapman, you're not right in the head—"

Johnny shook his head. "As people have been telling me all my days, Mr. Stadden—my father and stepmother, my brothers and sisters. Even my schoolmaster once told me I didn't have the sense God gave geese. But He made me as I am. I have never felt such purpose, such determination, coursing through my blood."

He balled his hands into fists. "God has told me what I am to do with my life. I've never known such peace. I—I can't describe it. This is my one true calling, sir. My life's mission."

"Mr. Chapman, have you at least flints to start a campfire?"

"Oh. I hadn't thought of that."

Mr. Stadden opened a drawer and handed Johnny a tin firebox. In it were flints, bits of cloth, and matches wrapped in greased paper. "Brown pine needles make good tinder," he said. "Flints, skill, and patience will start a fire. The matches are for emergencies. I'll pay you through the month of October."

"Keep your money, sir; God will provide. I've got no place to spend it in the wilderness."

"Mr. Chapman," Mr. Stadden said sternly, "I will pay you. I will not be a confederate to foolishness."

He opened a lockbox and stacked coins onto his sideboard.

"I have a brother, Isaac Stadden, in Licking County, Ohio. Do me the favor of calling on him. Tell him we're getting along fine. I may pay him a visit myself some spring, when we're not so busy."

"I will."

When Mr. Stadden shook Johnny's hand, Johnny was surprised to see real pain in the other man's eyes.

"I can't agree with what you're doing, Mr. Chapman. You're a good carpenter: skilled, steady, and strong. When you run out of apple seeds, come back to Pittsburgh. I'll take you back faster than two shakes of a lamb's tail."

"I understand. Thank you for your confidence, sir."

🍎🍎🍎

Johnny discovered he needed his salary after all. He bought two canoes, one for himself and one for apple seeds and provisions. He bought a saucepan, which would also serve as a rain and snow hat; another shirt; boots for winter; and a sack of cornmeal. He had Mrs. Van Kirk's Bible.

Johnny drilled holes in the canoes' gunwales and lashed them together with grapevine. He was ready to go.

🍎🍎🍎

Johnny lost track of the days almost immediately. He had been paddling for maybe two weeks when he lost the warm October weather as well.

One morning, he awoke to winter: bare branches;

gray skies; cold, slippery leaves on the ground; and a damp fog in the air. A blustery wind blew up the Ohio, making his wet clothes all the colder.

He thought about Mr. Stadden's hearth fire, and Mrs. Van Kirk's good cooking, all that day.

The next day he found a level patch of land, far enough from the Ohio's floodplain so as not to wash away, but not so shrouded with brush that the sunshine would have no purchase.

This is a good place! My very first apple orchard in the wilderness!

His heart pounded in excitement.

But in his zeal and haste to leave Pittsburgh, he'd forgotten to buy a shovel or trowel for the planting of the apple seeds. Johnny had to dig the holes by hand, a slow and painful task. His hands caked with soil. His bleeding fingertips soon turned that soil to mud. His hands began to throb.

He dug the holes as deep as his hand was wide and five strides apart. Three apple seeds per hole: one Ashram's Kernel hole for every three McIntosh.

"One for doubt under the hoe,
One to sprout, and one to grow."

By sunset, his feet were as muddy and cold as his hands after stomping the wet, cloying earth back into the ground. He walled in the nursery with brush to discourage foraging critters from eating the young apple trees.

It had taken him one whole day to dig thirty holes for thirty apple trees.

The air grew colder, yet Johnny lingered. The thirty patches of soil seemed filled with portent: The very earth seemed to tremble with energy. For the first time ever, the hand of man had planted something on this riverbank.

He could only marvel at the wonder of it. Some folks live an entire lifetime without making their mark on the world, without giving something back. With these thirty apple trees, Johnny had perhaps changed the world for the good. His heart filled with gladness and his voice with praise.

"For the first time since Creation," he said, feeling a bit foolish for calling out loud, "there will be apple trees growing on the banks of the Ohio River. A miracle. All the pioneers who come after me will have apples, from the very Tree of Life.

"'He which soweth sparingly shall reap also sparingly; and he which soweth bountifully shall reap also bountifully.'

"'While the earth remaineth, seedtime and harvest, and cold and heat, and summer and winter, and day and night shall not cease.'

"'This is the day which the Lord hath made; we will rejoice, and be glad in it.'

"Thank you," he shouted. "Thank you for my mission."

His voice echoed through the forest and sounded against the tree trunks. The squirrels and chipmunks were quiet for a moment, then burst into indignant chatter.

"You're angry," Johnny said to them. "Angry to have your quiet woods disturbed. I'll be on my way directly."

He realized, too late, that he'd wiped his bloody hands on his pant legs. The scent of blood would draw the grizzlies and big cats.

Johnny sighed. He'd have to dowse himself in the frigid Ohio.

🌳🌳🌳

On the Ohio side of the river, he hadn't seen one soul since leaving Pittsburgh. There was a long way to go before the first river town in Ohio—Marietta. Marietta had been named for the Queen of France, Marie Antoinette. Her little town was a pretty one, in her honor. Or so he'd heard.

Johnny was well under way when he thought of something. He lifted his paddle from the river in surprise: Did the people of Marietta speak English? He spoke not a word of French.

The wilderness was distressingly empty of people.

In the two years he'd lived in Pittsburgh, Johnny had

seen thousands of westering pioneers passing through on their way to the borderlands. They'd sell or dismantle their Conestoga wagons, pack up a broadhorn, and leave, the golden West a fire in their eyes.

So where was everybody? On either side of the Ohio, he saw nothing but steep riverbanks and heard nothing but wind blowing through the trees and the singing of wintering birds.

He planted apple seeds every ten miles or so on the Ohio side. Clearing the brush to prepare each orchard took at least a day. Just as Mrs. Van Kirk had suggested, he was careful to mix McIntosh and Ashram's Kernel.

It was hard to be a cheerful giver; Johnny was cold and lonesome. He daydreamed about Mrs. Van Kirk's sister and Mr. Stadden's brother.

If I could spend just one day warm and dry, and have a good night's sleep, I'd be so grateful.

The evening campfire cheered his spirit. He collected firewood when the sunset turned the Ohio to shimmering gold. He'd hang his wet clothes on sticks and watch them steam dry before his campfire.

Now the metal rain hat became a saucepan. As the corn mush boiled, Johnny added ashes from the campfire in lieu of salt. Eating in the dark was a powerful blessing, as his evening meal was surely the color of a gray squirrel's belly. Other than corn mush, Johnny watched what the squirrels ate and ate that. Nuts, mostly.

Before going to sleep, he'd dress again in warm, dry clothes.

If Johnny didn't sleep directly on the sack of cornmeal, the next morning the sack's mouth would be torn asunder, with swarms of snarling raccoons and opossums upon it, with their teeth bared and their muzzles dusted with cornmeal. Johnny would have to chase them off with a stick.

What if the same fate befell the apple seeds!

He learned to sleep with his head pillowed on the cornmeal sack and his feet stuck into the leather apple seed pouches. Even so, hungry critters would pester all night. They'd sniff at the cornmeal sack, their whiskers bristling against Johnny's cheek. He tried not to think about their sharp teeth tearing into his face.

Sleep was the balm of Gilead, but it did not come easy.

Once, he opened his eyes to a raccoon family staring right back at him. Their eyes gleamed in the moonlight. "I know what you want," he said. "'Ask, and it shall be given you; seek, and ye will find.'"

The raccoons stood up on their hind legs. Their whiskers quivered in alarm.

"But I can't give you a measure of my corn. I'm sorry." He closed his eyes again. He could feel them staring still. Eventually, the family waddled off.

Then one night, snow flurries hissed into his campfire. Johnny decided to stop planting for the season. The frozen earth would be impossible to break open with bare hands. There were no raccoons or opossums after that first snow. The forest was as quiet as the grave.

Now what?

Johnny found himself thinking more and more longingly of Mrs. Elizabeth Van Kirk's sister in Champaign County. Surely Mrs. Van Kirk's cheerful countenance and giving nature had been inherited by her sister as well.

After a snowy morning spent painstakingly picking the apple seeds off his bare feet and putting them back into the leather pouches, Johnny decided that he would find Mrs. Van Kirk's sister. In truth, he'd had no sleep the night before. The lean-to he'd built against the winter wind proved to be no blessing. Also, there was a scarcity of blankets and coats in the wilderness. His teeth would not stop chattering. His mind felt wrapped in thick, fuzzy wool.

If only I had that wool across my back and not in my head!

The snow was now over his ankles: Time for the blessing known as boots. He pulled them out of the bottom of his cornmeal sack.

Mrs. Van Kirk's sister would let him dry his clothes, rest by a fire, sleep on a dry floor, and wait until the spring to plant the apple seeds her sister had sent her. Johnny was sure of that.

There were no cabins from whence he'd come. But then, he'd been canoeing and walking the riverbank mostly. Farms were more likely inland, away from the Ohio's floodplains.

One morning he came upon a smaller river flowing into the bigger one. And praise be to God, on the other side of the smaller river lay a cabin!

This pioneer's homestead was a one-room shack built of logs and chinked with river mud. In his fields, great stumps of burned-off trees competed for space amid the yellowing cornstalks. Within a simple split-rail fence grazed a horse and cow. The air smelled of cook smoke, overlaid with the sickly-sweet smell of livestock manure. The pungent, salty scent of cured meat drifted from a smokehouse. And wonder of wonders, the voices of laughing children! His heart leaped in gladness.

Johnny stood in the line of trees, not knowing what to do. His clothes were caked with bloody mud. He'd been finger combing his hair since Pittsburgh. His beard was alive with critters, fleas or nits of some sort. He'd been clenching his teeth to keep them from chattering. Now his jaws felt frozen shut. He was cold to the bone.

His jaws unhinged, creaky and slow. "Good day to you all!" he shouted.

The horse bolted and ran. The cow chased after the horse in clumsy panic. Immediately a man stood in the doorway, rifle in hand.

"Good day to you all!" Johnny shouted again. "Might I have a word?"

"Git offa my land."

"Sir, I'm looking for both Champaign and Licking Counties. Either one near these parts?"

The man cocked his rifle and pointed it at Johnny. "I said, 'Git offa my land.'"

"I come as a friend, sir. I mean you no harm. Just . . . I'm just asking directions, that's all. I've friends in those counties. I'll be on my way directly."

The man hesitated. A half dozen faces fanned out behind him. Five children and their mother, Johnny reckoned.

"Perhaps you know them. I'm looking for a Mr. and Mrs. James Bushnell of Champaign County, or a Mr. and Mrs. Isaac Stadden of Licking County. I'd be powerfully obliged for directions."

The man stared for a long moment. Finally, he eased his rifle down and gestured with it toward the river.

Johnny hadn't realized he'd been holding his breath. He exhaled and tried a nod and a smile at the children.

The householder said, "This here's the Little Muskingum. You want the big 'un, west o' here. Follow it to Zanesville, then north-northwest to Licking County. Don't know yer folks there."

"And Champaign County?"

"Shoot. Champaign County's farther west o' here.

Might as well be Shawnee land in the Indiana Territory."

"Thank you very much, sir."

As Johnny stepped out of the line of trees, the house-holder pointed his rifle at him again.

"I'll be on my way now," Johnny said in as steady a voice as he could muster. "One more thing, sir. I've planted apple seeds upriver about a thousand paces. In seven years, it'll be an orchard. You'll have enough apples for you and your whole family to get through the winter. Then you can plant more apple seeds for more trees for your neighbors. Are you familiar with the parable of the loaves and the fishes, sir? Apples, a blessing four-thousand-fold."

The man's face darkened. "Ya planted 'em on my land?"

"No, sir," Johnny called out, praying to Heaven that he hadn't.

"Ya planted 'em on yer land?"

"Well . . . no. You could say that I planted them on God's land."

"If it ain't yer land, why'd ya plant them?"

"I planted the apple seeds for you."

A pause. "For me?"

"Someday you and your family will enjoy the apples. Save the seeds and I'll come back and do the planting, if you'd rather."

Slowly, the man took one hand off his rifle and scratched his beard with it. "If that ain't the durndest thing I ever heard. Yer plantin' seeds for *me* with no gain for *you?* Yer not right in the head, boy."

"So people have told me. God has made me as I am, sir."

The man stared, long and hard. He stopped scratching his beard. With two hands, he pointed his rifle just above Johnny's head and fired. The explosion shattered the still air. From somewhere behind the cabin, a flock of chickens burst into cackling. From within the cabin, a dog barked, low and mean.

Johnny took off through the trees heading north, and crossed the Little Muskingum far upstream.

I fail to understand! I fail to understand the low, ornery ways of men.

Well, some men.

He headed west toward the Big Muskingum and Zanesville. And, he hoped, a better reception at Mr. Isaac Stadden's house.

4

THE WINTER
1799~1800

Frozen wetlands are colder than frozen forest ground. At least, the wetlands *felt* colder. Johnny reckoned it was all that ice, stiff within the marshland soil.

He walked the frozen-solid swamps along the riverbanks of the Big Muskingum to Zanesville. The cold crept from the soles of his feet all the way to his knees. After a few days' walking, his legs were numb below his kneecaps. Yet another blessing, but it made the going all the harder. It was a curious feeling, as though he were kneeling his way through the wilderness, yet he could see his feet plain as day below him. The air was as cold and as dry as dust; he ate snow continuously.

By night, he'd have a campfire and cook his corn mush supper. His stomach growled as he packed snow into the saucepan, then waited for the melting snow to boil. It just took too long as the winter wind blasted against his face and against his hollow stomach.

He began to thrust his feet into the saucepan to melt the snow first. They were numb anyway, and the boiling went much faster.

He thanked God for his daily bread, ate quickly, and tried to sleep. As his benumbed feet began to warm, tucked within the leather apple seed pouches, the thaw felt like fire scorching his toes. But the pain would always pass; Johnny would focus his mind on the passing.

At dawn he'd awake and just lie there a spell, hugging his cornmeal sack to his middle, with his feet (finally) snug and warm in the apple seed pouches.

The trees thrust their bare branches into the pewter-colored sky. The ice-covered branches clattered like bones as the wind blew up the river valley. In the very center of the Big Muskingum, the water flowed fast and hard. Fisher hawks dipped and wheeled in the mist above the current. The sun rose milky yellow.

Johnny smiled at the redbirds as a cheerful contrast against the snow and the gray layers of stone, ice, trees, and sky.

The frozen world is harsh, but it's no use pretending that it doesn't have its own bleak beauty.

It took about a week to follow the bends of the Big Muskingum to Zanesville.

There a Mr. Ebenezer Zane and his good wife, Bessie, took him in. It was the Advent season and close to Christmas, they said. The spacious cabin, ample food, broad hearth fire, and many laughing grandchildren were powerful blessings.

Mr. Zane told harrowing tales of Indian fighting from his youth. "Those were the days," he sighed. "An adventure from one breath to the next. Now I'm just an old farmer with a head full of memories to keep me company. Life seems smaller, somehow."

"I prefer smaller," Bessie Zane said firmly. A grandson raced by, whooping like a crane. She scooped him up by the waist. "Noah, I know it's almost Christmas, but settle yourself."

"I've come out to the borderlands to plant apple seeds," Johnny told them. "Just three apple seeds will yield a tree; in seven years a tree will grow enough apples to feed a family through the winter. More apple seeds yield more trees with more apples: God has given me my mission in life—it will abolish hunger, and hunger will abolish want. Want will abolish warfare. 'The wolf also shall dwell with the lamb, and the leopard shall lie down with the kid.'"

Johnny braced himself for the familiar condemnations. There were none. Either the Zanes didn't consider his mission peculiar or they were too polite to say. He was astonished. Actual encouragement had never occurred before.

Ebenezer Zane nodded. "You speak the truth, John

Chapman, but save your apple seeds. There's no need to plant around here. My father planted an orchard when we were a pioneering family in Wheeling, on the Virginia side. I brought seedlings with me when we crossed the river 'bout twenty years ago. We have a fine orchard behind our cabin."

"Save the apple seeds, then, Mr. Zane. I'll return someday to fetch them."

The grandson Noah's dark eyes flashed, full of mischief. "Save the seeds for Johnny Appleseed!" he cried.

"Johnny Appleseed! Johnny Appleseed!" the other children echoed.

Their grandfather grinned at him. "It appears that's going to be your name from now on. At least around here."

"You may be right, Mr. Zane. Save the seeds for Johnny Appleseed."

🌳🌳🌳

It was the darkest time of the year, and darker still in the wilderness. Before he lit his evening campfire, Johnny would peer between the tree trunks and bare branches, searching for glimmers of cabin light. If he saw such a light, he'd head off thankfully in that direction in the morning. He figured that in that roundabout way, he'd meet up with the Staddens somehow.

The weather turned bitterly cold. Fresh snow blew off the branches and stung his face and neck. Caught in the wind, great flocks of dead leaves rattled and flew between the tree trunks. Pine boughs sighed against the gusts. Saplings shivered. The very earth seemed to tremble with the cold.

His breath froze to his beard in layers of ice. His frozen beard pinched and pulled the tender skin around his chapped and bleeding lips. It hurt to cough. It hurt to sneeze. It hurt to talk. Johnny took to clamping his mouth shut like a cabin door sealed tight against the winter.

Then he caught some sort of winter ague. Even the lightest of exertions would set him coughing with such force that he had to bend over to finish the job. When he finished, his face felt as though it had been stung by bees.

He was feverishly hot, yet cold at the same time. His muscles ached clear to the bone. His lungs wheezed with every breath.

He'd wake up in the middle of the night shivering and unable to stop, no matter how far he thrust his feet into the apple seed pouches, or how close he dared sleep next to the dying embers of the campfire.

He had a constant, sharp headache, as though someone had thrust a needle into his forehead.

Where am I?

Is anyone more alone than at night, sick and shivering in a winter wilderness? He'd lie awake, and entire evenings spent with his family in Longmeadow, Massachusetts, would roll before his mind's eye.

The Chapmans would speak as clear as a bell. He saw and heard them as though they were on the other side of the campfire. He just lay there watching and listening: In his feverish state, they were more vivid in hindsight than they ever had been all sitting together around the table. Another of God's blessings.

In the flickering firelight, his siblings spoke excitedly of freedom—of marriage, of the military, of merchant ships, of colleges, of apprenticeships, of teaching positions, of pioneering on the western trails, of the fur trade. They'd interrupt one another, each more thrilled than the last.

Why, they were as eager to leave home as I was!

And their parents? As the younger Chapmans spoke, their mother's shoulders drooped; their father sank even lower in his chair and reached for the applejack.

Will I ever see them all again?

Within the wee hours of night, when the soul is most alone, doubt crept into Johnny's thoughts, just as the bitter cold crept into his feverish limbs. Was this what the Lord had intended for him to do? Had he heard Him correctly? And if not this, what?

Should he go back to Massachusetts and take care of an aged father and stepmother? Presumably the half brothers and sisters were long gone. It was the eldest son's duty to care for the parents.

But what about the apple seeds?

How can I be sure? But how can we be sure of anything? Our plans, our foundations, our very roots, are they not merely driftwood we cling to in rough and unfathomable seas?

In the morning, he tramped the vast, silent forest with not one sign from God to keep him company. He was a voice crying in the wilderness: "What should I do? What should I do now?"

He received no answer save the occasional fisher hawk's cry and the sound of his numb feet tramping the snow. Not even the wind whispering through the pine trees gave him an answer.

Mrs. Van Kirk's Bible wasn't much help, either. He'd try to read and his mind would wander. Palm trees! Dates and almonds! Vineyards and olive groves! Figs and pomegranates! Sandals and tunics! Linen cloaks, tents, and camels! How hard could their lives have been, these men and women of the Bible? At least the Holy Land was warm!

One night, as the wind howled through the treetops, he whispered, "What should I do, Lord? I'm listening. Should I go back home? Are two pouches of apple seeds mission enough?"

He held his breath, waiting. His frozen beard

pinched and pulled as he set his mouth back into place. The wind howled louder.

But what about the apple seeds, and the loaves and the fishes? I can bring orchards to the borderlands. I can bring the apple, and its parable of charity and abundance, to these pioneering folk.

And yet charity begins at home, home in Massachusetts. It is the eldest son's duty to take care of his aged parents.

I'll go home in the morning. All right, then.

Johnny's tears froze on his face. His soul felt as darkly empty as the winter's night. His thoughts whistled round and round like the wind.

In the morning, he headed due east, east to Massachusetts, one foot plodding in front of the other all that day. Squirrels, rabbits, deer, moose, then bears, then finally demons glared at him from behind the tree trunks. Their eyes were angry fires that gave off no heat.

For the first time, Johnny felt scared. What if he died? Alone, right here in the middle of the wilderness? What if years and years of autumn leaf fall roiled his flesh into earth, his bones to dust? What if no one found him ... ever?

In a blue and silent twilight, with the snow hip-deep, a light burned vivid orange. Not a bear! Not a demon! A cabin!

In his haste, he tripped over tree roots and crashed, elbows first, through the ice into a freshet. The ice and frigid water shocked his feverishly hot limbs and brow.

This had to be Mr. Isaac Stadden's homestead!

"Mr. Isaac Stadden!" he shouted. "I bring news of your brother, Mr. Joshua Stadden, of Pittsburgh!"

The man of the house, rifle at the ready, opened the door. "State your name and business."

"My name is John Chapman, and I worked for your brother in Pittsburgh. If you are Isaac Stadden."

The rifle barrel drifted downward. "I am. Come in."

Johnny staggered to the hearth fire. A wife and two children watched, their faces becoming more astonished by the moment. He pressed as close to the fire as he dared. His clothes unfroze and commenced to drip, then hissed with steam.

Staddens flew around in the steam, and the steam became mist. Staddens dipped and wheeled like the fisher hawks over the Big Muskingum.

"Fisher hawks," he said. "You're all fisher hawks."

They flew up into the sky (no, the ceiling), and that was all he remembered.

🌳🌳🌳

He awoke to the crunch of a cornhusk mattress below and the weight of many blankets above. And he was still cold.

"Mr. Chapman?" Mrs. Stadden called through the fog.

"Yes?"

"Why are you here? Do you have something to tell us about my brother-in-law?"

"He's well." The cabin walls turned black.

"Mr. Chapman? Mr. Chapman?" It was Mrs. Stadden again.

"Yes?"

"If Joshua is well, why are you here?"

"To plant apple seeds."

A pause. "Apple seeds?"

"For you, and for all the people in the borderlands. How—how long have I been here?"

"The first time you fainted, you lay here for three days. The second time, two days."

He struggled to get up. "I should take my leave. I have people to see. The Bushnells of Champaign County."

"You'll do nothing of the sort." Mrs. Stadden pushed his shoulders onto the bed. "You almost died, Mr. Chapman. We were going to put you in the smokehouse till the March thaw."

"The smokehouse? Why?"

"We could not have buried you till then. The earth is frozen, Mr. Chapman."

"Is he awake?" Mr. Stadden asked. He bent over the bed, his face tight with worry. *A good man! Just like his brother!*

"Yes, but the poor soul is incoherent." She turned to

her husband and whispered, "The snow has drifted to the eaves and he's babbling about apple seeds! Raging fever has addled his brain, fried it like an egg!"

Mr. Stadden shook his head. "The poor man."

"I'm fine," Johnny whispered, but they didn't hear.

Mrs. Stadden said, "I've rubbed a poultice upon your chest, Mr. Chapman. Bear grease mixed with mint leaves and cloves to arrest the coughing and ease congestion. Are you able to take some nourishment? I have broth waiting."

"Thank you." He pulled himself up onto his elbows. When Mrs. Stadden spooned some broth into his mouth, he fainted.

"Mr. Chapman?" It was Mrs. Stadden's voice in the fog again.

"How—how long did I faint this time?"

"Since this morning."

"First three days, then two days, and now since this morning. I reckon I'm getting better."

The children giggled.

Mr. Stadden bent over the bed again. "Mr. Chapman, since you're going to be with us this winter, perhaps you could take on some of our chores? There's firewood to chop, hogs and chickens to feed. The straw in my horse's stall needs to be turned over and aired. If and when you're able."

"Of course. I've always earned my keep."

Johnny spent his first winter in the wilderness with the Staddens of Licking County. After a long convalescence, he cleaned sties, stalls, and chicken coops. Using Mr. Stadden's carpentry tools, Johnny made a sled for the Stadden children, Thomas and Helen. Johnny could hear them whooping and hollering on the hills.

Johnny whittled raccoons, bears, and horses for Thomas. For Helen, he whittled a doll family complete with parents, a son and a daughter, and a babe in arms.

In April, he planted apple seeds around the Stadden property, three McIntosh trees for every Ashram's Kernel. His leather pouches were empty.

"I'll go back to Pittsburgh and work for your brother again. In the autumn I'll get more apple seeds from the cider presses south of there."

"You are a singular man, John Chapman," Mr. Stadden said. "All this way, all this time and trouble, just for apple seeds."

"It was the Zanes of Zanesville who started calling me Johnny Appleseed."

"Johnny Appleseed you shall be. Come back and see us anytime."

"Why, thank you. I'll do just that."

Mrs. Stadden refilled his bag of cornmeal for his

sojourning suppers. The children waved. Johnny waved back.

🌳🌳🌳

He'd hidden his canoes in a lea. They were covered in sodden leaves, as sticky as wet ashes. Squirrels and chipmunks had used the bows and sterns as caches for acorns, chestnuts, and black walnuts.

The canoes were in good shape, considering. Johnny scooped out the nuts with both hands and set them on dry land. With his fingernails, he scraped the decaying leaves off the gunwales.

He put in and set out.

The paddling was much harder going upstream: He hadn't thought of that. The trees along the riverbank leafed out as the spring slowly ripened. Trillium covered the forest floor in blossoms bright as milk. The tender grass in the glades looked good enough to eat.

Deer families gathered at the riverbank to drink. As the canoes slipped by, they looked up in alarm, ears twitching, water dripping from their muzzles. Johnny paddled farther into the Ohio's mainstream. The paddling was harder still, but he didn't want to frighten the deer.

There was no one on the river.

Pittsburgh hadn't changed one whit. The fisticuffs, the grudges, the permanent bad blood—it was like a twenty-four-hour-a-day dogfight.

54

On a warm spring afternoon Johnny knocked on Mr. Joshua Stadden's front door.

"God in Heaven!" Mr. Stadden exclaimed. "John Chapman! You're alive!"

"Good afternoon, Mr. Stadden. I've spent the winter with your brother, Isaac. He and his wife are well, with two children and another on the way. Might I work for you again this spring and summer? I'll go to the cider presses in Elizabeth this autumn for more apple seeds."

"Excellent. I can put you to work immediately."

Johnny was taken aback. "Might I rest first? Some food?"

"Time is money, Mr. Chapman. Have you forgotten?"

He sighed. "I had forgotten."

Mr. Joshua Stadden appeared taken aback as well. Only then did it occur to Johnny what he must look like: Pants tattered to ribbons, his one shirt long gone; his feet cracked and bleeding at the heels, the blackened toenails as long and curved as bear claws.

His hair and beard were greasy, matted, and crawling with nits. His skin was speckled gray with dirt and campfire smoke.

Johnny grinned at his employer. "My mission is not an easy one."

"Perhaps a bathe in the river first, Mr. Chapman?"

Mr. Stadden said politely. "My wife will fetch you some soap, and a hot meal after. Then back to work: Flatboats, Mr. Chapman, for the restive pioneers."

"Yes, sir."

II

~

EXODUS

A Circle of Friends
1800

"Mr. Van Kirk, do you remember me?"

It was a sweet October day, and Johnny was standing in front of the presses in Elizabeth, Pennsylvania. As it had the year before, the crisp, golden air smelled of apples and cider.

Mr. Van Kirk and two cider men heaved a barrel of apples into the press. "Did you work the crush last year?" Mr. Van Kirk asked.

"Just the one day. I took your apple seeds and planted them in the western borderlands. I've come back for more. Look."

It was Johnny's custom to tie Mrs. Van Kirk's Bible around his middle with a rope. He pulled it out.

"This here's the Bible your wife gave me last autumn. It got me through many an evening, Mr. Van Kirk, cold and alone. She could not have given me a better gift. I read it by campfire light, sometimes by moon- and starlight."

Mr. Van Kirk stared, his mouth as big and round as an apple. "Elizabeth!" he shouted. "Come out here! You won't believe this."

Mrs. Van Kirk stepped out of her cabin door, wiping her hands on a dishcloth. She hadn't changed a bit. Her hair was still the same warm brown as a female cardinal's feathers, her forearms still as thick as a man's.

Mr. Van Kirk grinned at his wife. "Look who's here, Elizabeth."

Johnny said, "Mrs. Van Kirk, how are you?"

Mrs. Van Kirk frowned. "You look familiar, sir."

"I tried to call on your sister, Mrs. James Bushnell, but Champaign County is far from here. I'll try again this season. I'll need more of your Ashram's Kernel apple seeds to plant around her cabin, if that's all right."

"As I live and breathe," Mrs. Van Kirk said. "You're alive! How many times did the mister and I sit in front of the hearth fire last winter, figuring all the different ways you could die out there in Ohio? Indians. Wolves. Bears. Panthers. The winter itself without even a coat on your back."

"You . . . you wanted me to die?"

"Of course not! It's just that—"

Mr. Van Kirk tapped his forehead with a meaningful look.

"Cease, William." Mrs. Van Kirk pursed her lips. "I'm sorry, sir. I don't remember your name. John something?"

60

"John Chapman, but folks in the borderlands have been calling me Johnny Appleseed. I've come for more apple seeds, if that's all right."

Mrs. Van Kirk said, "You're welcome to as many seeds as you like. After a good meal."

🌳🌳🌳

Mrs. Van Kirk had made another bountiful supper, with apples served in all manner Johnny could think of: stewed, fried, chopped, sugared and spiced, sauced, in pies, in dumplings, in crisps and cobblers. The cider men, the Van Kirks, and Johnny ate for a long time without speaking.

"Where is your son, Mr. Van Kirk?" Johnny asked after his second helping of apple cake. "Last year he was here, working the presses alongside you."

The Van Kirks exchanged glances. Husband nodded to wife, and she spoke. "Willie has gone east to New Haven, Connecticut. He's attending Yale College and reading law there. I know pride's a sin, but we're just so proud of him!"

"That's wonderful news. Of course you're proud of him. I will tell the Bushnells when I see them."

"Thank you, Johnny Appleseed," Mrs. Van Kirk said, taking his plate. "Have some more cake."

🌳🌳🌳

For this year's mission he bought a shovel, a heavy wool coat, and a Hudson's Bay blanket of sturdy wool. The rest of his salary he gave to a poor pioneering family. Without it, they would surely have bought one of Mr. Tubman's disreputable flatboats. Just the thought of their flatboat sinking, and those precious children pulled under by the Ohio's implacable current, made him wish he'd given them all his money.

If he could survive last winter's sojourn without such luxuries, did he really need a coat, blanket, and shovel this year? Perhaps not, but he'd already bought them.

Just as he had last year, Johnny stored his canoes in a lea. He was careful to make no noise at the mouth of the Little Muskingum. He saw the man who had shot at him the year before. The farmer was turning under his patch of earth with grim determination. The wife and children trudged slowly behind, pulling up cornstalks.

The farmer's dog peered at Johnny keenly; the ruff of fur around his big neck rose slowly, thick as a lion's mane. He lifted his upper lip to show off his teeth.

For one terrifying moment, Johnny thought he'd have to make a run for it. Then a rabbit caught the dog's attention. With a bark loud enough to open a dead man's eyes, the dog chased the rabbit, not Johnny.

🌳🌳🌳

Instead of going to Zanesville, Johnny crossed the Little Muskingum at the narrows and turned northwest, planting apple seeds along the way. This year Mrs. Van

Kirk had given him McIntosh, Ashram's Kernel, and another type of seed as well, Northern Spy.

Just as he had last year, he planted three seeds to a hole as deep as his hand was wide; three McIntosh plantings for one Ashram's Kernel and one Northern Spy. Just as he had last year, he felt compelled to extract a ceremony from the occasion when he was finished for the day, declaiming to the woods:

"One for doubt under the hoe,
One to sprout, and one to grow.

"'This is the day which the Lord hath made; we will rejoice, and be glad in it.'" Just as they had last year, the squirrels and chipmunks chattered indignantly.

In deepest winter, he felt that familiar prickle in his lungs. Another ague was coming.

How far was he from Champaign County? He had no idea.

One night, Johnny came upon a huge hollow log half buried in the snow. A powerful blessing! It would make a cozy bed for the night. Perhaps he could fight off the ague this year with God's help.

He made a hasty campfire and cooked his cornmeal mush with ashes. As the last embers died, he crawled into the log.

His hands came up against something soft and

warm in the darkness. He felt bones under fur, which was wiry and coarse. A wave of fever and fear washed over him and set his limbs to shivering.

A soft *whumpt* filled the dank air; after the *whumpt,* a whimper.

Another whimper. Something licked his nose.

What on earth?

Bears.

Hibernating bears—a sow and cubs were sleeping in this log!

Johnny shot out of there like a ball out of a cannon.

He watched in horror as a great paw reached out of the log, the claws glinting in the starshine. The paw twitched as though swatting at a bee.

He tore through the forest every which way. It was a coughing fit, and not the sow, that caught up with him and forced a stop. Johnny spent the night huddled against a tree.

The next morning, he followed his tracks back to the log to gather his apple seed pouches and baggage. Another powerful blessing: The bear family was fast asleep.

🌲🌲🌲

Many an evening he peered painstakingly through the trees, looking for cabin light. There was no such light to be seen through the blowing snow.

Then, one black evening, he did see a cabin light, south-southeast and over a creek. He followed the creek to a tiny lone cabin with a much bigger barn attached. The snow-laden wind caught a wisp of smoke, pulling it skyward from the chimney.

The heavenly scent of freshly baked bread filled the night air.

One thing Johnny had learned: Always announce yourself from the safety of the trees.

He shouted, "Mr. and Mrs. James Bushnell of Champaign County?"

A man appeared in the doorway, rifle in hand. "State your business."

"I'm John Chapman. I know your sister-in-law and her husband, the Van Kirks of Elizabeth, Pennsylvania. If you are the Bushnells? Might I come in?"

"We are. You may."

Johnny wove his way out of the forest and stepped across the threshold. Mrs. Van Kirk stood before him! The same dark eyes and warm brown hair, the same forearms as big as a man's!

"Mrs. Van Kirk," he stammered in astonishment. "Why—why aren't you in Pennsylvania?"

The woman's eyes filled with tears. "I'm her twin sister. My name is Esther Bushnell."

Johnny commenced to cough and leaned over.

"Please sit down by the fire, Mr. Chapman. Have some hot sassafras and cherry-bark tea. It does wonders for a fever and cough. I've just brewed a pot."

Sipping his tea, Johnny could feel himself growing stronger by the moment. The Bushnells of Champaign County! How many times had he thought of this cabin, a safe harbor from the storm? And God be praised, here he was. He looked around the cabin in wonder.

"Your cabin," he said. "Everything's neat as a pin."

Esther beamed at him. "My husband calls me house-proud, Mr. Chapman. And yet it has always been my contention that a good farm wife should never let the farm into the farmhouse."

"I can't tell you how many times I've thought of your homestead, and here I am! In the very heart of the wilderness."

"The very heart of the wilderness?" Mr. Bushnell echoed in amazement. He jerked his thumb, pointing south. "Cincinnati's only a three-day ride from here."

"Cincinnati!" Johnny exclaimed. "I forgot all about Cincinnati!"

Mr. Bushnell leaned forward eagerly. "I've just returned from there, with all the news."

"James," Mrs. Bushnell said sharply, "leave the poor man alone. He's sick."

"Champaign County . . . it's an odd name," Johnny mused.

Mr. Bushnell settled himself more comfortably. "It means level, open country. Tell me, sir, what have you heard of the Jefferson-Burr campaign?"

66

"James, don't start in on that," said Mrs. Bushnell, just as Johnny asked, "Jefferson Burr? Who's he?"

Mrs. Bushnell groaned.

Mr. Bushnell looked astounded. "The presidential election campaign of last November! Thomas Jefferson won the election fair and square, but Aaron Burr would not concede and demanded recount after recount of the votes. The Jefferson camp kept saying, 'The votes have been counted, sir, once, twice, three times! Pack up your tent and concede, sir.' But the Burr camp wouldn't hear of it."

Mrs. Bushnell sighed. "All he wants to talk about is that fool election."

Johnny said politely, "That's all right, Mrs. Bushnell. I pay little attention to politics. This is a chance to catch up. So . . . who's the president now?"

Mr. Bushnell gaped at him. "Thomas Jefferson! In the Electoral College, sir! Mr. Alexander Hamilton could see for himself who was the better man. He changed his vote from Aaron Burr to Thomas Jefferson in the Electoral College! President Jefferson won by one vote."

"Mayhap it's my fever—I don't understand, Mr. Bushnell. The election was tied before Mr. Hamilton changed his vote? But didn't you say before that Mr. Jefferson had already won it fair and square?"

"He's the better man!" Mr. Bushnell was shouting now.

Mrs. Bushnell shouted, too, "James! Enough!"

Mr. Bushnell said, "You astonish me, Mr. Chapman. I vote to represent Ohio. Surely you do the same?"

"Well, you see, Mr. Bushnell, I don't own land anywhere. I don't live anywhere. So in fairness, I can't represent anywhere. I've never voted in an election."

"You . . . don't live anywhere?" Mrs. Bushnell echoed.

"I live under the sun, and the moon, and the stars. Or rather, I live under God's angels. The stars, you see, are God's angels. I talk to them at night, and they talk back to me. Many a night I don't sleep a wink. The conversations we have! You might say I represent the angels, not that they have much to say about politics.

"Two of them especially," Johnny went on in a fond voice. "They've introduced themselves to me just this winter. They're a powerful blessing against the cold and the solitary life I lead.

"We're betrothed, the three of us. That is to say, if I don't marry in this life, they'll be my brides in the next. They're more spirits than angels, truth be told, for they walk next to me by day and talk to me by night. Oh, the love we share! 'Beloved, if God so loved us, we ought also to love one another.'"

Mr. and Mrs. Bushnell exchanged uneasy glances.

Johnny stood up in shock. "Their names, Mrs. Bushnell! Their names! My spirit-wives' names are

Esther and Elizabeth! Just like you and your sister! The four of you have the same names!"

Mrs. Bushnell's left hand flew to her throat. Mr. Bushnell's glance flitted to his rifle by the door.

Silence.

Johnny stammered, "I've—I've talked too much. I spend so much time as a solitary, I remember, too late, the rules of social discourse. You're not the first people I've frightened with talk of my spirit-wives."

Mrs. Bushnell's hands commenced to tremble. Tea sloshed onto her lap.

"Now I've really scared you. I'll leave."

"Mr. Chapman, that's quite all right," she said quickly. "You know the Bible?"

"I bring news fresh from Heaven. Why! I have something to show you!"

Mr. and Mrs. Bushnell leaned back, wild-eyed and wary, as Johnny pulled a rope from round his middle. He caught the Van Kirk Bible just before it hit the floor.

"Your sister gave this to me before my first sojourn in the wilderness."

"Our mother's Bible," Mrs. Bushnell said with a throb in her voice. She put down her teacup and took it in her hands wonderingly.

"I should give it to you," Johnny said, "if it was your mother's."

"No, no, Mr. Chapman. My sister meant for you to have it," Mrs. Bushnell said stoutly. She brushed away tears. "My sister is a good judge of character. She must have seen much good in you."

"You're absolutely certain?"

The Bushnells exchanged glances. "We haven't had a visitor in months, Mr. Chapman. We can't read: It would give me great pleasure to hear you read the Good Book aloud."

"Read!" Johnny jumped into the air and crowed like a rooster. "I forgot to tell you! Your nephew Willie has gone to New Haven, Connecticut, reading law at Yale College."

Mrs. Bushnell dropped the Bible into her lap and clapped her hands. "Oh, that is good news! Willie at Yale! I haven't seen him since he was a baby."

"I'll read your mother's Bible as long as you wish to hear it, but I mean to head south as the weather warms. Your sister gives me apple seeds every October. I promised her I'd plant Ashram's Kernel seeds round your house. That's your sister's favorite apple. I'll plant Northern Spy as well. Then I'll plant more apple seeds down Cincinnati way."

Mr. Bushnell slapped his knee. "I've heard of you! You're all the talk of the Ohio, upstream and down. Johnny Appleseed?"

"That is what folks call me."

Mrs. Bushnell patted the bench. "Please, Johnny Appleseed, sit down. Read us Bible verses if you're able. I've just baked bread. You do sound as though you have a bad cold. You're welcome to stay as long as you like."

6
ANOTHER CIRCLE OF FRIENDS
1801

April is the best time for planting apple seeds. The sun warms the thawing earth, and the earth warms the seeds. The everyday miracle begins again.

It was late April or early May, and Johnny was wandering through the forest looking for a good place to sow apple seeds. He'd spent the morning under a pine, taking shelter from a cloudburst.

Now the spring sunshine warmed his face. The wet, chilly breeze smelled of flowers. The trillium, the wild violets, and the red clover—the wilderness was full to bursting with life.

Among the evergreens, the lovely planes of the dogwoods glowed purest white, even as the redbud trees glowed purest red.

Johnny spread his arms wide: "'He shall come down like rain upon the mown grass: as showers that water the earth.'"

He walked right up to a shagbark hickory sapling just to admire the leaf buds. Above these buds was a bird's nest. To Johnny's shock, the mother bird just sat there gazing down at him, without a hint of fright.

In Massachusetts, birds had long since learned to be afraid of people, what with all those generations of boys with slingshots. But here in the wilderness, this mother bird had no more fear of him than she would of a tree.

A calm, fearless bird! Finally, a sign from God after all these months of waiting! The wilderness is a second chance, a rebirth, the pioneering folk learning from mankind's mistakes! The New Jerusalem!

"You're not afraid of me, are you, little bird?" he asked in delight. "It's not too late for us, then, is it?"

The mother bird cocked one eye at him, then the other.

Johnny fell to his knees, his arms outstretched. "'Here am I.' Thank you, Lord!"

It was at that moment that the trees moved. *The trees moved.* Was there no limit to His signs, His wonders to behold? Quick as an eye blink, the mother bird flew away.

The tree trunks surrounded him.

It was only then that he noticed the war paint and feathers, the moccasins and breechcloths. These men were the very color of the tree trunks.

They hoisted him to his feet.

"God loves all and prefers none," Johnny said, as they tied his wrists together with a leather thong. Two of them had the apple seed pouches slung around their necks. Another carried the cornmeal sack and shovel.

They gestured that he should walk. And they did, in a westward direction. He wasn't afraid: If it was his time, then His will be done.

I've planted orchards aplenty. My spirit-wives, Esther and Elizabeth, are waiting.

The sun was just dipping toward sunset when they arrived in a village. People rushed out of their longhouses to walk alongside. Some of the men held clubs made of gourds. These they brandished above Johnny's head, their faces hot in anger, their dark eyes flashing.

A white man came forward. He smiled at Johnny, but his green eyes looked as cold as frozen pond water. Florid face, bad teeth, and bloodshot eyes—Johnny knew the signs of a heavy drinker.

The man shook his head in mock sympathy. "What were you thinking, trespassing on Seneca land?" he asked. "Yer name?"

"John Chapman."

"I expect you know who I am."

"No, I don't, sir."

The man looked startled. "You've never heard of me? Simon Girty? The notorious traitor to his own race?

The man no decent white family will abide at their table?"

"I don't know you, Mr. Girty. And I condemn no man."

"Is that right? Well, sir, these Seneca are about to condemn you to death. See the two lines they're forming? That's called the gauntlet, Mr. Chapman. You'll run between them, and they'll hit you just as hard as they can. With war clubs, burning logs, yer own shovel—anything they can get their hands on.

"If you run fast, you'll just prolong yer agony. Yer best bet is to submit an' git yer misery over with as soon as possible. Heaven awaits, or so they say."

Simon Girty nodded to an old man standing before them. "This gent's name is Chief Gyantwaka. The whites call him Cornplanter. This here is his town. This is New Deonosadaga. The original town was seven days east o' here. It was destroyed by the American army, two years ago. Yer in Indiana now, no Ohio law here to save you."

He turned to Johnny and spat out his words in fury. "This is Seneca land and yer about to pay the price. Everyone in that gauntlet lost somebody in the Deonosadaga Massacre, includin' me. You got anything to say that might save yer hide, Mr. Chapman?"

Two women upended the leather pouches, dumping their contents to the ground.

Johnny looked at Cornplanter and spoke in a shaking voice. "I travel the wilderness to plant apple seeds, sir. Those are apple seeds. I've come this way to plant them, nothing more. If—if you'll give me my seeds, my cornmeal, and my shovel, I'll be on my way.

"Or . . . or I could show you how to plant them. There's a little poem about it, passed down through the ages:

"One for doubt under the hoe,
One to sprout, and one to grow.

"We'll plant an orchard, Mr. Cornplanter, as far as the eye can see. You'll have apples in seven years, plenty for all your people to get through an entire winter."

Johnny stammered on, stammered to save his life. "And . . . and enough to trade, to trade with your neighbors."

Just because I'm certain of the next world doesn't mean I want to leave the blessings of this one. I reckon I'm not so rarin' to join Esther and Elizabeth after all.

"Tell them the parable of the loaves and the fishes, Mr. Girty. If you give away everything you have, you have more, not less."

Simon Girty sighed. "That yer best shot, Mr. Chapman?"

There must have been one hundred people, fifty a

side, on the gauntlet. They were all glaring at Johnny, even the children. He'd never seen such hatred, not even on the faces of the brawling lumbermen back in Pittsburgh.

"It is. No, wait! Tell them … tell them this."

Johnny took a deep breath to ease his pounding heart. "Tell them that apple trees grow best when there are two different kinds of trees growing together: McIntosh and Northern Spy, or McIntosh and Ashram's Kernel.

"Aren't people the same way? That is, if two different kinds of people live in the same place, don't they make each other stronger? They are nourished by each other's strengths *because* they're different. Would you tell them that, Mr. Girty?"

Mr. Girty looked him over for a moment, rubbing his jaw. He shrugged his shoulders and spat. "Well, all right."

Simon Girty talked loud and long—in the Seneca language, Johnny reckoned—and he stood in one place and spread out his arms, like an apple tree. Simon Girty talked and talked.

Cornplanter narrowed his eyes at Johnny. When Simon Girty stood in another place and stretched his arms even wider, the Seneca looked surprised. They asked questions. Simon Girty nodded his head vigorously and talked and talked. The Seneca people asked him more questions and ran the apple seeds through their fingers.

Finally, he stopped talking. The Seneca turned their

77

faces as one to look at Cornplanter. He studied Johnny. After a long silence, it was the war captain himself who threw the blade of his tomahawk into the ground. The blade sank through the soil like a knife through butter.

"I remember apples," Cornplanter said.

Johnny tried hard to contain his shock.

Cornplanter could speak English!

Surely he would have been no more surprised had a bear walked right out of the wilderness and begun speaking to him.

"There are many orchards around Niagara and Buffalo," Cornplanter said. "Do you know these places? These towns are near Seneca land in New York."

"I've heard of them."

Cornplanter went on. "Apples are good medicine. Is it true? Apple trees grow stronger, their fruit is sweeter, when there are different kinds growing together?"

"It's true. Just like people, in my opinion."

"You wait."

Cornplanter called five men together. They squatted in a group around a campfire and talked. One by one, the gauntleteers joined the gathering around the campfire and listened. They began to argue among themselves; they seemed to have forgotten all about their prisoner.

The twilight ended; darkness closed in. The campfire grew brighter.

"Do you know what they're saying, Mr. Girty?"

"Yer hide is saved, Mr. Chapman, but this is the most confounded foolishness I've ever heard of. You risk your life to plant seeds?"

"Could you untie the thong, Mr. Girty? My wrists have been throbbing since noon."

"That ain't my place, Mr. Chapman. I'm a guest of the Seneca, just like you are. What about yer wife? Yer children? What do they think about you wandering the wilderness, alone and unarmed?"

"I don't have a wife or children." Johnny decided it would not be a good idea to mention the spirit-wives at this point. "It wouldn't be fair to a family, Mr. Girty, what with me gone all the time. God has given me this mission as His great gift. Apples will abolish hunger, then want, then warfare; for once we all have enough to eat, there won't be a reason to fight with one another anymore."

"I expect yer Johnny Appleseed. Yer the talk of the frontier, sir, and almost as famous as myself. I figured you for a made-up tall tale, like the Green Knight, or that Golem feller, or the giant on the top of Jack's beanstalk. Ever hear of Dick Whittington's cat?"

"I'm real."

"Cornplanter is about to offer you dinner. There's a venison-and-raccoon stew."

"I'll thank him for it, but I don't eat meat, Mr. Girty. Corn, squash, and beans will suit me fine."

"I heard you was strange. No rifle, not even a knife. You spout Bible verses by the hour and wander the wilderness, talkin' to the animals and to spirit-wives. Don't look so surprised, Johnny Appleseed. Word travels fast, especially on a frontier.

"Spirit-wives!" Simon Girty roared in laughter. "Ain't you got nothing to say? Ain't you gonna defend yer sorry manhood?"

Johnny said softly, "Thank you for saving my life."

Simon Girty's whole demeanor changed. The smirk left his face, he hung his head. "I'm sorry. The solitary life is a hard one. We have that in common. I—I lost my whole family in the massacre. I admit to talking to them," he whispered, his voice breaking. "I talk to them all the time." He took a knife out of his shirt and cut the thong from Johnny's wrists.

"Cornplanter wants to plant apple seeds with you, startin' tomorrow. Yer an honored guest of the Seneca, for as long as you wish to be. He's over there right now, talking about giving you safe passage among the neighbors. The Shawnee, the Wyandotte, and what's left of the Delaware live right here in Indiana now.

"And yer welcome to come back, anytime."

🌳🌳🌳

For the next ten days, Cornplanter, the Seneca men, Simon Girty, and Johnny cleared away brush, then dug two hundred holes for two hundred apple trees.

Johnny stayed in Cornplanter's longhouse. The Seneca women stood in line to give him vegetable stews and dried-berry soups.

When Johnny wasn't digging, he set the Seneca children to laughing, once they figured out that he used his saucepan both for cooking and as a hat. He borrowed a knife and whittled animals for them.

The children told him stories, which Cornplanter translated into English.

The planting was finished. Too soon, it was time to leave. All the Seneca gathered round. They looked expectantly at Johnny.

He stood over the newly planted orchard and knew at once what to say.

"'Behold, how good and how pleasant it is for brethren to dwell together in unity! It is like that precious ointment upon the head, that ran down upon the beard, even Aaron's beard.'

"'Praise him with the sound of the trumpet: praise him with the psaltery and harp. Praise him with the timbrel and dance: praise him with—'"

"Looks like rain, Johnny," Simon Girty interrupted, smiling.

Johnny laughed. "I expect I can take a hint from you, Simon Girty. Cornplanter," he said, taking the war captain's hands, "I will never forget your kindness to me. You'll have more than enough food for your people.

I'll come back seven years hence, I promise. I'll show you the best ways to prepare and store your apples."

"Johnny Appleseed," Cornplanter said softly. The deep creases in his ancient face stood out clearly in the brazen sunlight. The wrinkles in Cornplanter's face drew downward into deep lines of sadness.

He took a deep breath. "We won't be here when these apples are ready. We will never gain by these, for I feel the coming of the whites is inescapable. I do not begrudge your foresight for them."

"No, no, Cornplanter! You don't understand. My mission is for the Seneca as much as for the whites. With apples, there is more than enough for all."

"For your sake, I hope I am wrong. The Seneca have lands in New York, Pennsylvania, and Ohio. Wherever we are, you are always welcome. Please find us.

"My granddaughter has a gift for you."

A little girl handed Johnny a small earthenware cask corked with a wooden stopper.

"This is walnut oil," Cornplanter said. "Rub it onto your hands, feet, and lips, and they will not dry out and crack this winter. Nothing is better than walnut oil."

"The precious ointment of unity." Johnny's eyes brimmed with tears. "Thank you, Cornplanter."

THE RICHFIELD NONESUCH
1805

Captain Elijah Welton wore his tricorn hat in the house, a holdover from his years as an army officer. Battered and moth-eaten from years spent outdoors, the once-crisp black felt now looked like a gray tabby dozing on his head.

He leaned forward eagerly, his keen blue eyes glowing in excitement. "Mark my words, Mr. Chapman. War is coming, and that means our main chance. Britain will have her hands full fighting Napoleon in Europe. We can control the Great Lakes *and* annex Canada right under the Prince Regent's nose!"

Johnny gazed into his teacup and nodded. He'd spent years listening to old soldiers spin war stories by the fire. In each yarn the old soldier's actions were always—always—the ones that stole astonishing victory from the hands of sure defeat.

Captain Welton hadn't been in the army since the

Revolution, and yet he still called himself captain. How could the horrors of wartime be the defining moments in a man's life? All that terror, hunger, and hardship— you'd think he'd want to forget about it as quickly as possible.

"That doesn't seem fair, does it?" Johnny asked. "If Spain, Flanders, and Russia need Britain's help, we shouldn't try to take advantage of their generosity."

Captain Welton sputtered. "Generosity and warfare have nothing in common, sir!"

"You're right. I pay so little attention to politics. Still, my schoolmaster used to tell us about the grand cathedrals of the Old World. Wouldn't it be a shame if those beautiful churches were destroyed? Wouldn't it be worse if America had a part in it?"

Captain Welton turned as red as a cranberry pudding. "Churches and warfare have nothing in common either. It'll be the war to end all wars this time."

He glared. "More than enough glory for those who have the courage to fight. I remember when I was baggage wagoner to General George Washington...."

Johnny and Captain Welton were sitting in front of the kitchen hearth of Aaron Miller's cabin. As Captain Welton told a long, complicated story about the Battle of Yorktown, involving missing couriers and his own vaunted courage, Johnny looked out the cabin window and admired Miller's Corners.

Surrounding the cabin, as though his home were a ship tossed by shimmering waves of corn and wheat, lay Aaron Miller's abundant fields. Next to the barns, the sheepfold and paddock were crowded with fattened livestock. On the west side of the cabin, poplar saplings shot up to the sky as a fence against the winter's snow and wind. A sugar bush covered the surrounding hills.

Far in the distance, Aaron Miller tended his crops, staggering behind a team of oxen. Even farther in the distance, the Cuyahoga River roared, full to overflowing with winter runoff and spring rains, on its way north to Lake Erie.

"And that's how we won the Battle of Yorktown!" Captain Welton shouted triumphantly. He looked at his listeners with that gleam in his eye that people have when they are expecting praise.

"That was a fine piece of bravery, Captain," Mrs. Zilla Miller said. Captain Welton drained his tankard. "It's no wonder General Washington was so taken with you, Captain."

Johnny could tell from her voice, sort of faraway yet soothing, that she hadn't been listening to him either.

Captain Welton gave them a little moo of satisfaction.

"This is a beautiful farm, Mrs. Miller," Johnny said to his hostess. "Miller's Corners is always one of my favorite stops."

"Mr. Miller and I are from Hartford, Connecticut, Mr. Chapman. Someday we'll build a fine brick house on this land. It is our dream to have a farm that looks as though it were right in the middle of the Constitution State."

"I'm from Massachusetts. I haven't seen a fine brick house in I don't know how long."

He turned to Captain Welton. "My father fought in the Revolution as well, sir. Nathaniel Chapman was a minuteman. As you said, there's more than enough glory to go around."

Captain Welton looked at Johnny with new respect. "Your father was a minuteman?"

"He was at Lexington and Concord on April nineteenth, 1775."

Already Johnny's heart was pounding. Already his mouth felt dry. He never spoke about his father, never. The male battle! Foolish, foolish pride! But it was like closing the barn door after the horse gets out. As Mrs. Miller and Captain Welton voiced their encouragement, his mind, too late, raced to change the subject.

"My half sister lives in Mansfield, in Richland County, now," he said. "It's a peculiar thing—we weren't close at all in Massachusetts, but I've spent the last four winters with Persis and her husband, William Broom. She's the only one of my siblings who moved to Ohio."

He rushed on, as fast as the Cuyahoga rushing in the

distance. "It's taken some getting used to, having neighbors so close. Just last winter I saw the man next door sitting in front of his own fire reading his newspaper. I could just make out the headlines. For a man who spends his life in the very heart of the wilderness ... well ... it's a marvel."

"He must live in Ohio, then!" Mrs. Miller exclaimed. "By that I mean your father. A war hero would surely have taken up the government's offer of free land here in the Western Reserve."

"He lives in Washington County, near Marietta."

"How very curious." Mrs. Miller frowned. "He needn't have bought a farm near the Ohio River when he could have had land for free right here. He could have had his very own town—Chapman's Corners."

"He likes the weather down there," Johnny mumbled. "My sister—"

"The weather? In *Marietta?*" Mrs. Miller's hands fluttered to her throat. "Floods in spring, hordes of mosquitoes and rattlesnakes in summer, and ice storms in winter? Marietta might as well be Pharaoh's Egypt during the Plagues. What could he have been thinking, Mr. Chapman?"

Johnny had planted apple seeds just last April around his father's cabin and farm. Well, not really a farm, and not even a cabin. Nathaniel Chapman was a squatter, on land owned by a man who lived in New Bedford, Massachusetts.

Now that Johnny's stepmother was no longer alive to prop Nathaniel up, Johnny had been shocked to see how quickly, and how far, his father had fallen down. Nathaniel Chapman's home was a one-room shack, practically a lean-to. He hadn't bothered with windows; the only light came through gaps between logs in walls he hadn't bothered to chink. His only hog ran wild in the forest. No crops, not even a kitchen garden. Broken jugs reeking of corn squeezings littered the floor he slept on. And he slept most of the time.

Will he be alive in seven years, when the first crop of apples is ready?

What a blessing it was that his stepmother was buried in Longmeadow. Living in such conditions would have broken her in two.

He said quietly, "I've never known what my father was thinking, Mrs. Miller."

She hesitated for a moment, her eyelids fluttering— then turned to the window and peered out.

"What fine weather we're having!" she announced, her voice full of polite encouragement. "Is there anything so rare as a day in June?"

Johnny spoke eagerly. "It's a lovely day. Perfect apple seed planting weather, don't you agree, Captain?"

There was a little hitch, the smallest change in the air. The danger had passed. Women! Johnny marveled. How did they do it? Surely they were God's greatest blessing, for they knew, unfailingly, what to say or do in any situation. Their courtesy was instinctive, God given, for it took a man years and years to learn such a skill. Most men weren't even aware that such a skill existed.

Surely the best people on this earth are the best of women, just as the worst of us are the worst of men.

"Don't bother planting any of your apple seeds around here," Captain Welton announced. "Are you still planting that McIntosh, Mr. Chapman?"

"And Ashram's Kernel, Northern Spy, and my favorite, the Rambo."

"Bah!" The captain scowled. "None of them will survive the winters out here in the Western Reserve, sir. You'd best stick to planting out orchards in the Ohio Valley. Your varieties are not hardy enough for these parts."

The captain fixed a steely gaze on Johnny. Johnny knew what that meant: *Just like your apples, Mr. Chapman, you're not hardy enough for these parts, either. Or any parts, come to think of it.*

"That isn't true, Captain," Johnny replied. "I've had great success here and in the Firelands to the west. My seedlings have excellent roots and sound trunks. I've planted on both open land and in Quarter Sections."

"Firelands? What is that? And what are Quarter Sections?" Mrs. Miller asked.

"If a Connecticut soldier lost his farm to the fires of

war, Mrs. Miller, the government will give him richer, flatter land farther to the west, out Sandusky way. That's the Firelands.

"As to Quarter Sections. Well." Johnny took a deep breath.

"'I, John Chapman, by occupation a gatherer and planter of apple seeds'—that's what I always write on land deeds, Mrs. Miller. A lot of folks—lawyers, sheriffs, homesteaders, and judges mostly—want my comings and goings written out. As though quill and paper were as hard and fast as chisel and stone, or as firm a foundation as apple seeds and the good earth.

"I'll ask the homesteader if he'll lease to me one fourth of his homestead. I agree to pay the homesteader with apple trees once the nursery grows: Forty trees per Quarter Section."

Johnny sighed. "This is the part of my mission I don't like. I don't mean the payment in apple trees. I mean sometimes I have to wait weeks for a circuit judge or circuit lawyer to arrive at the nearest town."

"The law can be a muddle, Mr. Chapman."

"I can lose months of good planting, Mrs. Miller, just waiting for the law to give me permission to plant. I prefer planting on God's land. He needs no witness save me."

"God's land." Captain Welton grinned at Johnny. "It be God's land, sure enough, but the state of Ohio expects its taxes, doesn't it?"

"Taxes?"

"On the land you've claimed for nurseries," Captain Welton replied. "One third of the money I collect for seedlings goes to taxes."

"Money?"

A pause. "Surely you collect money for your trees, Mr. Chapman?"

"No. My mission is to have the trees already here, for when pioneer folk come out to the borderlands. Why should they buy the apples God has given them as a blessing?"

Captain Welton looked at Johnny as though for the first time. "You don't ... pay any taxes?"

"I don't own anything. God meets all my wants, not the state of Ohio. The apples are God's gift and my mission."

"Any apples yet on those trees?" Captain Welton demanded.

"It's too early to tell."

"You won't have a one, Mr. Chapman. You mark my words. Now, *my* apple ..."

Captain Welton teetered his chair forward on two legs, reached across the table, and shook his finger under Johnny's nose. "The Richfield Nonesuch— there's an apple! Excellent for pies and all sorts of stewing, excellent for cider, excellent keepers, too. You can't do better.

"My family is still in Connecticut, but when I bring Mrs. Welton and our children out here, our orchard will be nothing but the Richfield Nonesuch."

"You should have two or more kinds of trees in your orchards," Johnny replied. "Variety makes them all stronger."

The captain slammed his chair down on the ground. "Bah! An old wives' tale! Indian legends!"

"It was I who taught the Seneca to plant that way!"

Mrs. Miller said firmly, "Mr. Chapman, have some more wild-grape pie. You, too, Captain Welton. These grapes have been sweetened with our own maple sugar." She slid huge slices of pie onto their plates. A few bright-purple grapes rolled onto the table.

"Oh dear, I'll need a fresh towel. Please excuse me, gentlemen."

She wagged her finger at them cheerfully, and yet Johnny could tell from her snapping eyes that she meant business. "I don't want to hear any more squabbling about apples! And no more talk of taxes, either. Mr. Miller won't abide such talk in his house."

"Of course, madame." Captain Welton stood up, clicking his heels together. Johnny hitched himself about halfway out of his chair. Mrs. Miller went outside to fetch a towel from her drying rack.

The captain sat down again and leaned forward in

his chair. "Now that the lady of the house is gone, Chapman, I do have a bit of news to share. This sort of business upsets the ladies, you understand."

Johnny picked up his spoon.

"A year ago this July eleventh, Aaron Burr called out Alexander Hamilton, demanding satisfaction. They met at sunrise: Now Hamilton is dead."

Captain Welton looked at him expectantly.

"He demanded satisfaction for what?"

"Chapman! Don't you know anything about the manly arts? Aaron Burr challenged him to a duel! A duel, Chapman! Burr ran against Thomas Jefferson for the presidency five years ago."

"Oh, yes, I remember. My good friend Mr. James Bushnell of Champaign County said something about Mr. Burr refusing to concede the election. . . ."

"Mr. Hamilton changed his vote to Thomas Jefferson. Mr. Hamilton once said he considered it his duty to stop Aaron Burr's career at every opportunity. Now Burr has stopped his."

"So what's happened to him?" Johnny asked. "Is he in jail?"

"Last I heard, he was hiding out on an island in the middle of the Ohio on the Virginia side—on Herman Blennerhassett's estate. He's wanted for murder in New York and New Jersey."

"How long can Mr. Burr hide out on an island?

Surely President Jefferson can call a militia of some sort, have him arrested."

Captain Welton barked a short, bitter laugh. "Burr is still the vice-president. One would assume he has federal duties to perform."

"Why is he wanted in two states?"

"The duel took place in New Jersey. His estate is in New York. Shoot, Burr used to be *governor* of New York! He can't go back now."

Mrs. Miller's face appeared in the cabin window.

"This not paying taxes is a bad business, Chapman," Captain Welton said in a quick, low voice. "Do your duty, man, as painful as it may be. The law will catch up with you someday. It always does."

Their hostess entered the cabin. She dipped a fresh towel in a bucket of water and wiped around their plates.

"More tea, gentlemen?"

The captain said, "Thank you so kindly, madame."

She poured tea, and they ate and drank in silence.

"Here's a thought," Johnny said after a bit. "Governors, presidents, even kings: They live, they die, and their power and glory dies with them. But think of the apple, Captain Welton. The apple trees we plant today will live for one hundred and fifty, maybe two hundred years. And with grafts and scions, our trees will live forever."

Captain Welton's mouth fell open in surprise. Purple grape juice ran down his chin. "Right you are, Chapman," he said, wiping his face with a napkin. "Kings are dust! Presidents are nothing compared to us!"

"Compared to the apple, you mean."

"The apple, right." The captain put his spoon down. "I'm going to create a new variety of apple. The Welton Pie apple! Of course! It'll be the best apple under Heaven! You'd be wise to create the Chapman. It won't be as delicious or as hearty as the Welton Pie apple, of course, but—"

"You've misunderstood me, sir. The glory is in the apple."

"Captain Welton, everyone knows Johnny Appleseed," Mrs. Miller broke in. "People will remember his name for as long as there are apples. Won't they, Mr. Chapman?"

"Oh, no. Not me—"

"They'll remember Captain Elijah Welton, too," the captain interrupted loudly. "Baggage wagoner to General George Washington, inventor of the Welton Pie apple."

"Of course they will, Captain Welton." Mrs. Miller gave Johnny the sweetest smile under Heaven. "More pie, Mr. Chapman?"

8

A Trumpet in the Wilderness
1812

"Here they are!" a soldier shouted from a rampart in Fort Findlay. "General William Hull, I salute you!"

The apple seeds Johnny had planted out in the Firelands, near Fort Findlay, sent shoots swiftly from the ground, as though they couldn't wait to bear fruit. It was his favorite place for planting.

He and the others in front of the fort—women, children, old men—turned their faces northward and waited expectantly.

After a bit, a man on horseback rode out of the clear summer air and, behind him, a long line of men.

General William Hull, Governor of the Michigan Territory and Indian Commissioner to Canada, rode tall in his saddle on a splendid bay horse. Both man and horse looked the crowd over regally, with deep nods of both heads to the left and right.

Johnny was surprised by General Hull's age. Long

white hair flowed behind him, as bespoke a cavalry officer. Why hadn't the government commissioned a much younger man to be commander of the western forces?

Long gone were the tricorn hats of Johnny's youth, for both military and civilian wear. General Hull wore a tall peltry hat that looked like a stovepipe with a short brim in front. A dusty white feather drooped from the top.

Behind him marched a militia, mostly Ohioans and Kentuckians, judging from their banners, and twelve hundred strong. The men had marched downstream from the Maumee River, past the Black Swamp and into Fort Findlay.

"Huzzah! Huzzah!" the crowd roared.

General Hull stopped, turned his horse around, and stood right in front of Johnny. "You're Johnny Appleseed, are you not? You have to be—with that waist-length beard and hair."

Johnny stood up straighter. "I am. I can't go anywhere these days without being recognized. Such is the price of fame, I suspect. May I be of service to you, General Hull?"

"You may. I have just received my orders from President Madison in Washington City. We are to proceed to Detroit and attack the British there. I have my orders to annex Lower Canada as quickly as possible. You may help me, for you know the byways in these parts better than any man. I need a scout."

Johnny's heart sank. "Why attack Canada, General Hull? What have the Canadians done to us?"

"Indeed. In point of fact, I have a brother with a farm on the Thames River near Lake St. Clair in Ontario. But we must invade Canada to keep the British from invading us."

"Have they announced that intent, General? Captain Elijah Welton once told me that should there be a world at war, the British would be too busy fighting Napoleon in Europe to engage in battle here."

General Hull dismissed Johnny's protestations with an impatient brush of his hand.

"A soldier has his orders. I need a scout," he repeated.

Captain Welton was right, seven years ago! The government will use a distracted Britain as an excuse to invade Canada.

"I know the Firelands of western Ohio and eastern Indiana, true enough, but I don't know the byways of the Michigan Territory, General," Johnny said in as firm a voice as he could muster. "I've never planted apple seeds north of here. I've never been to Detroit or Frenchtown."

General Hull gave him a long, hard stare. "Do you refuse?"

Johnny took a deep breath. "No, General. But I can't be of any help to you. I'm sorry."

General Hull, there have always been wars and battles and such. But there has to be another way! It's the other way I believe in.

"Very well, then." General Hull wheeled his horse around and rode magnificently into Fort Findlay. A mighty roar welled up among the citizenry as the rest of the militia followed him. The main gates, made of the tallest, noblest of oaks, slammed shut with a boom.

🌳🌳🌳

Two months later, Johnny sat in the shade of a sycamore, taking his ease creekside in the steamy heat of an August noon. He had just spent ten days planting out apple seeds on the Wabash River near Fort Wayne, Indiana.

The stiffness in his lower back and shoulders surprised him.

I must be getting old. I've never had aches and pains before. I'll be thirty-eight next month—that's still a young man. Maybe the agues I catch near every winter have finally caught up with me.

A man on horseback galloped by, his mount lathered two inches thick with sweat. He and Johnny locked eyes for just a moment before he hurried on.

Quick as a bullet he was back.

"Who are you?" the man demanded, pulling his horse down to a stop.

Johnny stood up. "My name is John Chapman."

Both man and horse were breathing hard. Heat radiated from the horse's brisket, and long strands of foam drooled from his mouth. The sweat on the man's brow had streaked to mud on his dusty face.

"You're that Johnny Appleseed feller, ain't you?" the man asked. "You wander the wilderness. You know these parts?"

"Folks call me that. I have wandered the wilderness these thirteen years."

"We need your help." The man leaned over and spat mud out of his mouth. Only then did Johnny notice that he was wearing a dusty army officer's uniform.

"General Hull surrendered Detroit to the British, to General Brock."

"That's wonderful news. The war is over!"

"No, it isn't over!" the officer shouted bitterly. "Tecumseh's Shawnee are on the warpath, moving fast into the Michigan and Indiana Territories. Into Ohio as well. The citizenry need to be warned."

"I know this patch of Indiana like the back of my hand," Johnny replied quickly. "I've got Quarter Sections everywhere. I know all the stations, all the cabins. Follow this path straight south, sir. You'll come across hundreds of settlements."

"You head east, Mr. Chapman. Tell everyone you come across to run south, head for the Ohio River. Run for their lives."

"Sir, the Ohio is days away! There's a fort and blockhouse in Mansfield, Ohio. That's about due east of here.

As you head south, tell them all to run north-northeast to Mansfield."

"That I will," the man replied grimly. "Good luck."

He wheeled his horse around and dug his right heel into his flank. He was a cloud of dust before Johnny could wish him good luck as well.

The nearest cabin due east was Meadows Station. Johnny took off at a run, but his cornmeal sack, apple seed pouches, and shovel slowed him down. So did his Bible, which kept slipping out of the rope tied about his waist. He had to stop more than once to pick it up from the forest floor.

The Meadows family was in the fields.

"Abner! Ophelia!" he shouted. Father and mother stopped in their tracks, as did their many children.

"Johnny Appleseed, whatever is wrong?" Ophelia Meadows called out. "You look like you've seen a ghost."

He was breathing hard. "The Spirit of the Lord is upon me . . . and he hath anointed me to blow the trumpet in the wilderness . . . and sound an alarm in the forest; for behold . . . the tribes of the heathen are round about your doors, and a devouring flame followeth after them."

Stunned silence. Abner Meadows asked, "What did you say?"

"The Spirit of the Lord—"

"Confound it, Johnny! English!"

"Yes, the English, Abner, or rather the Shawnee ... General Hull has lost Fort Detroit.... They're spilling south, creating havoc everywhere. The blockhouse in Mansfield is your only hope."

"Boys!" Mr. Meadows shouted. "Hitch up the wagon! Now!"

"Abner, might I leave my cornmeal, apple seeds, shovel, and Bible with you? I've been pressed into service by the army to warn the citizenry."

Abner Meadows replied, "Of course you may. But no army asked you to warn the citizenry like that."

"Like what?"

"Johnny, speak plain English! 'East to Mansfield! The Shawnee are coming! Detroit is lost!' Warn folks like that! Don't waste time with fancy Bible speechifying!"

"Oh. I hadn't thought of that."

The Meadows family packed up a few changes of clothes, some pots and pans, and themselves. Johnny tossed his possessions into one corner of their wagon just as Abner was tying his cow to the backboard.

"We'll see you in Mansfield, Johnny. Remember what I said."

"Yes, Abner. Godspeed. If you can, warn my sister and brother-in-law, Persis and William Broom. They live in Mansfield."

"Hyah!" Abner shouted, with the crack of the whip. The oxen groaned and pulled forward. Abner and

Ophelia's many children sat in stunned, silent terror in the wagon.

Johnny ran past them, through Claxton's Station, Wheeldon's Station, Graham's Station, and past the Butler, Hessel, and Faulkner farms.

He took to announcing the particulars first: "The Shawnee are coming! Detroit is lost! East to the fortress in Mansfield and hurry! To Mansfield!"

By the time he got to "the tribes of the heathen are round your doors," they were loading their crying children and dusty clouds of squawking chickens into their wagons.

The full moon and starlit skies were a powerful blessing as Johnny ran south-southeast all through the night. He ran without ceasing, stopping only to pound on doors and shout through open windows.

"The Shawnee are coming! Detroit is lost! East to the blockhouse in Mansfield, and hurry! The Spirit of the Lord is upon me...."

By noon the next day, he was well into Ohio, circling southeast. He wound his way through Bucyrus, Sulfur Springs, and finally Mount Vernon, a voice crying in the wilderness. He stopped only to gulp water from streambeds.

The next afternoon he stretched out facedown in a deep stream and let the cold, rushing water sweep over him. Tiny fish darted away, quick as birds on the wing. Long, feathery tendrils of grass, bending to the current like saplings to the wind, clung to rocks in the streambed.

How long had the rocks lain there—smooth, mute, and oblivious to the terrors and sufferings of men?

No time to think about that now. He dragged himself out of the stream and took off again, running.

He shouted at farmers in their fields. He shouted through windows at families having supper before their hearth fires. He shouted at women spinning thread on their front porches.

"He hath anointed me to sound the trumpet in the forest! To the blockhouse in Mansfield! Go north! North! The Shawnee are coming! The Shawnee! The tribes of the heathen are round your doors."

What was that smell? The devouring flame! A terrible odor of burning cabins, spilled blood, and burning flesh filled the forest air. The heartbreaking scent of brother against brother!

And what was that . . . the screaming of terrified children?

"I hear the whispering of many, 'fear on every side!'"

The very air choked with smoke and horror. It was hard to breathe.

Johnny stopped in his tracks.

"James and Esther Bushnell!"

Champaign County was due west of Licking Creek.

If he moved fast, if he could just get that second wind, he could be at James and Esther's homestead by nightfall.

The Bushnells will be my last stop. The Shawnee wouldn't dare raid south of Champaign County. Surely they'd be too close to Cincinnati to take that risk.

He ran, leaping over logs, darting in between great stands of oaks, maples, beeches, and buckeye trees. There were no animals. Perchance they sensed the danger and hid, well within the peaceful confines of the deepest forest.

"Esther and Elizabeth, help me!" he shouted. "The Bushnells need our help!"

🌳🌳🌳

Was it the spirit-wives, Esther and Elizabeth, who pushed him along, lifting him over logs and disentangling him from thickets and thorny bushes?

At any rate, he ran west, in a burst of speed. The setting sun cast long shadows amid the tree trunks. Above the trees, the sunset glowed as red and orange as a wildfire.

There! The Bushnells' ridge! James's sugar bush! There was James's sugarhouse, patiently waiting for the next spring. There was James's smokehouse, waiting with equal patience for the solid cold weather of autumn to arrive.

The sunset blazed orange against a smudge of cook smoke, drifting above the line of trees.

Johnny ran up the ridge, already shouting, "James! Esther! To the blockhouse in Mansfield! Detroit is lost! The Spirit of the Lord is upon me—"

It wasn't cook smoke.

The Bushnells' home was burned out, the roof collapsed. James's horse was gone. His five pigs, throats cut, hides blistered, smoldered in their fenced pen.

It was absolutely quiet. Where were the chickens, clucking sleepily from the henhouse? Where were the birds, announcing the end of the day with drowsy trills? Where was Esther, crying into her apron? Where was James, rifle in hand?

"James! Esther! It's Johnny! I've come to warn you as a trumpet in the wilderness!"

As Johnny ran toward the cabin, a deep-throated growl vibrated through the darkening air. A mountain lioness slunk out of the cabin, with her belly to the ground, for something heavy dragged from her mouth: something long, smoking black, and spilling entrails onto the scorched earth. She locked her yellow-eyed gaze into Johnny's and growled again.

Another pig?

His blood froze.

"No! No!" he shouted. "Leave him!"

Johnny grabbed the first thing he could, a smoldering fence post, and threw it with all his strength.

It struck behind her ear. With an angry snarl, the lioness dropped her burden and ran into the forest.

🌳🌳🌳

He found a shovel and buried his dear friends quickly, lest the lioness steal back that night. He covered the shallow grave with singed planks from the Bushnells' beloved front door. He heaped more dirt on the planks.

Only then did he sit down to rest. Three days and three nights of running nonstop—where had such strength come from? He was too tired to think.

The full moon rose again. The stars, God's angels, twinkled as they had for nights uncountable. As they would continue to twinkle for nights uncountable.

"I want to be a stone," Johnny said bitterly. "I want to be a smooth, mute stone—oblivious to the terrors and sufferings of men."

He lay on the forest floor. "Why?" he shouted at the top of his voice, not caring if the Shawnee heard him or not. "'I cry in the daytime, but thou hearest not; and in the night season, and am not silent.'"

A night wind arose and cooled the air. The smoke rolled away, revealing a clear, star-filled black night, like a slab of obsidian held close to the firelight.

There were more stars than he'd ever seen before. More angels than he'd ever seen before.

"Esther! Elizabeth!" he screamed.

Don't you see, Johnny? James and Esther are with us now. As you will be someday. And all those children you heard? They're here with us, too. All of them are here.

"When?" he shouted. "When will I be with you? Esther! Elizabeth! I want to be with you now."

That day will come. You'll know it. You need to plant your apple seeds. Sleep now and take safety tomorrow. You'll be all right.

"I'll go to Mansfield tomorrow," he murmured. His eyelids were like lead weights, pulling downward. His back and shoulders began to hurt again. The soles of his feet felt on fire.

How could I not have noticed my aches and pains?

Johnny stared at his feet in astonishment. The soles were as tough as elephant skin, but now they were bleeding. He hadn't even noticed.

He'd been as unaware of his own discomforts as if he had been a star, or a stone, or an angel himself, these last three days and nights.

He hadn't eaten in days and didn't even feel hungry.

His limbs jerked and twitched, then lay still. He drifted toward the smooth, mute oblivion of sleep.

9

NEW DEONOSADAGA
1812

The next morning Johnny walked right into the Bushnells' streambed. He stretched out facedown in the current. He came up for air and drank and drank of the cold, sweet water. He rubbed his limbs with handfuls of wet sand.

Slowly, slowly, the grime and dirt from the last three days washed clean from his skin, hair, and beard.

The birds were back, singing their thanksgiving for dangers passed.

The faint scent of baking bread led him into the Bushnells' burned-out cabin. It was Mrs. Bushnell's starter: the flour and yeast mixture she had used to start her bread loaves. The starter had baked in the heat of the burning cabin. It had swelled, then overflowed the bowl she'd always kept it in and spilled out onto the dirt floor.

Already the field mice, as bold as brass, were gnawing on it.

Esther Bushnell had once said to him, "A good farm wife never lets the farm into the farmhouse." Johnny could almost see her before him, broom firmly in hand.

Mice in Esther's spotless kitchen! They would have made her furious.

He swept the mice and their droppings away and commenced to eat. The starter was awful. A thin crust on the outside; raw, yeasty sour, and fizzling on the inside. It smelled of burned cabin and mouse.

But his stomach seemed to leap up at the chance to eat something, anything.

As Johnny swallowed, the tears, finally, came to his eyes. Esther Bushnell had had the baker's gift. She could turn any flour, even the coarsest of stone ground, into the airiest, lightest bread.

His tears salted the starter.

He had nothing, not even his Bible.

Should I go to Mansfield with the others and join them in the blockhouse? The Meadowses must have gotten to safety. Surely my cornmeal sack, apple seed pouches, and Bible are safe with them.

More importantly, he needed to know if his sister and her family were safe. He needed to see familiar, living faces smiling back at him.

Cornplanter!

"I'll talk to Cornplanter," he said aloud. "I'll ask him

to ask the Shawnee to stop the raids! They'll listen to him."

He stuffed the starter crusts into his mouth and stepped out into the front yard. Only then did he notice that James's fields and orchard were untouched, as was his Quarter Section of apple trees.

The Shawnee will come back here and harvest the corn and apples for themselves. A few McIntosh, but mostly Ashram's Kernel, all the way from Turkey by way of Elizabeth, Pennsylvania.

"Esther! Elizabeth!" he called out. "South-south-west to New Deonosadaga! Help me run!" He took off at a run but stopped after a few paces. He was too achy, too tired, too heartsore, *too old,* to run today.

It took all Johnny's strength to walk the four days to Cornplanter's town, New Deonosadaga, in the Indiana Territory.

What do two hundred apple trees look like, cut down and burned in their fourth fruit-bearing year? The year's apples, just weeks away from harvesting, lay helter-skelter in blackened, still-steaming lumps on the ground.

What do three Seneca longhouses look like, burned beyond saving? There was no one, no one at all in the town.

New Deonosadaga looked like the end of the world.

"Cornplanter! Are you there? It's Johnny Appleseed!"

One by one, Seneca came out of hiding from the woods. They all sat down in the ruined orchard and cried together. Even that tough old bird Simon Girty sat on the outskirts and cried and cried.

"It was a Kentucky militia," Cornplanter said between keening wails. The others began to wail with him. Their sorrow sounded like the wind moaning across the bare branches of a winter forest.

Johnny thought back to his Massachusetts schoolmaster's lesson about Hadrian's Wall. It had been built of stone, in the north of England, almost two thousand years ago. Hadrian's Wall had not been built by the Scots to keep the Roman legions out of Scotland. Rather, Johnny had been surprised to learn, it had been built by the legions themselves, to keep the Scots out of the Glory of Rome.

The Scots used to paint their faces blue for battle, and they drank the blood of their slain enemies for strength. Sometimes they mixed the blood with grain, roasted it on a stick, and ate that. Caesar's soldiers had been scared beyond death of them.

Horror, misery, despair, and hopelessness leaped up within Johnny's heart like those blue-faced, bloodthirsty Scots. They'd finally breached his wall; the Hadrian's Wall he'd built around himself was not tall enough, or stout enough, to keep them from scaling it. Not this time.

"Where will you go, Cornplanter?" Johnny asked, wiping his eyes with the back of his hand. "Whatever will you do?"

Cornplanter took his time collecting himself before speaking.

"We had three years of fruit, and I thank you for that, Johnny Appleseed. These winters have been good, because of all the apples we had to eat.

"We'll go home. There is good Seneca land in Pennsylvania, on the northern banks of the Allegheny River. We'll live there."

Johnny whispered, "I'm not strong enough for my mission, Cornplanter. Another terrible war, and the apples have changed nothing. God put me here to change the world: The world has not changed one bit. I've failed Him utterly. My whole life is a failure."

Cornplanter looked at him. "Our Shawnee friends told me you ran from settlement to settlement, from farm to farm, warning them about their raiding parties. Their warriors tried to catch up with you. They said you ran without stopping for three days and three nights. One hundred and fifty miles, maybe more. The Shawnee are a proud people, not easily impressed. They're impressed by you.

"If you hadn't planted all those orchards, you would not have known where all those people lived.

"And living in the wilderness has made you strong,

113

as strong as any Seneca warrior. Who would have run, for three days and three nights, in your place?"

Johnny replied bitterly, "Now I've got the Shawnee on my tail?"

"I gave you safe passage years ago. You are wrong about your mission. Your apples have changed everything, Johnny—everything but the human heart.

"We found some apple seeds that weren't burned. We'll plant them around our new home. We will plant orchards and corn. My name is Cornplanter, after all."

Johnny looked at the blackened, scorched earth, with tendrils of smoke still pluming out of it. He whispered, "'The pomegranate tree, the palm tree also, and the apple tree, even all the trees of the field, are withered; because joy is withered away from the sons of men.'

"'Mine eyes do fail with tears.'"

Cornplanter said, "No one has ever looked into the heart of the Great Spirit. Perhaps your mission is just beginning. Perhaps, at this moment, the Great Spirit is testing your strength and resolve."

"Then He would find me wanting. I've spent thirteen years in the wilderness for nothing. Nothing!"

"Think of all the good you have done, and that will lighten your heart. You are welcome to visit us in Pennsylvania. Johnny Appleseed, you are welcome anytime."

III

THE KINGDOM

Fox and Wolf
1836

After thirty-seven years of gathering and planting apple seeds, Johnny knew what a perfect campsite, and a perfect camp, should be.

Near a fast-flowing creek for the clean water, but far away from a swamp because of the snakes, mosquitoes, and black flies.

A slight ridge for his bed—that way, if it rained in the night, he wouldn't be flooded. If he could find a tamarack, he'd strip some branches off and sleep underneath them in the summer. Nothing worked better to ward off mosquitoes. Even on the hottest, muggiest evening—even if it hadn't rained in weeks and the mosquitoes were ravenous—they would stay away.

He carried the tamarack branches with him until they turned brown and were bereft of needles. Then he used the bare branches for kindling.

He knew to peel wet wood until he got to the dry

core. He knew to stack the kindling just so, with plenty of air underneath for a quick, hot fire. He'd had to replace Mr. Joshua Stadden's flints three times—a new set of flints every twelve and a half years.

He knew just how much water to put in his saucepan for his cornmeal supper. He knew just how long to cook it. He knew just how much ash to add to the pot in lieu of salt.

He knew he could read his Bible until the first of the peepers came out. If he read until the hoot owls announced themselves, he'd have eyestrain and a headache the next day.

The lark woke him at dawn, as sure as a rooster.

He'd learned years before that the saucepan he wore in the rain and snow was no blessing in the heat of summer. In fair weather he stored it in one of his apple seed pouches.

More important than anything else, if the night was clear and the moon was down, he had to have a campsite with a full view of the stars. He talked to the stars and the stars answered back, just as though they were his family around his campfire.

The stars sang to him, with music more beautiful than the bluebird's song.

My life hasn't changed, he thought as he lay down for the night. His joints creaked and popped. These days, the muscles in his back and shoulders were knit painfully tight all through planting season. His fingers were stiff and achy, and as gnarled as hickory twigs.

Well, I reckon my body's changed. He grinned up at the stars.

But more than that, it's the world that's changed around me.

Just this afternoon in Vincennes, Indiana, he'd seen a miller's mule. He hadn't seen one of those since he was a boy in Massachusetts!

Hitched to the top half of two grinding stones, the miller's mule walked round and round and round and round in a circle, as the grain between the millstones was ground into flour. The animal had worn a path ten inches deep. The mule had a cloth around his eyes, so he would remain undistracted by the world.

Johnny walked a circle too, albeit a much larger one. Just as that miller's mule had walked for years on end, grinding grain into flour, so had Johnny walked round and round for years on end, planting seeds to grow into trees.

He went to Elizabeth, Pennsylvania, in the autumn to gather apple seeds, then westward bound through Ohio, planting seeds along the way. He always stayed with his half sister Persis and her family in Mansfield through the winter.

When the cold weather broke, he planted apple seeds through Indiana and Illinois. Sometimes he crossed the Mississippi and planted in Iowa. The few times he was in Missouri, he crossed again where the Mississippi and the Ohio met and planted in Kentucky.

Every year he thought the same thing: This year I'll follow the Mississippi far north to the Missouri, just like Lewis and Clark and the Corps of Discovery.

But then the dawn would break cold on the prairie one morning and his feet would be drawn eastward, pulled like a magnet. The second half of the circle would begin, back to Elizabeth, Pennsylvania, as the year drew to a close.

I'll walk the Missouri next year. It will be there, waiting.

The Missouri, the Mississippi, and the Ohio . . . Johnny thought of them as an immense apple tree, with the Mississippi as the trunk. This nation was one vast floodplain of the Mississippi River. He could only shake his head at the wonder of it. Rivers began draining into the Mississippi as far to the east as central Pennsylvania, and as far to the west as the Shoshone's country in the Rocky Mountains; thousands upon thousands of river miles.

The Mississippi River might as well be God Almighty, what with the lives bound up in her, what with the trust people put in her. No matter how much water people took out for farming, for drinking, for washing the dishes or the laundry, for cleaning their teeth, there was always more than enough water left.

The more water they took out, the more water remained, especially during the late-winter floods. The loaves and the fishes once again.

God as She? God as a River? Johnny smiled. Plenty of folks would call that blasphemy. To Johnny, it was the best praise he could think of.

As he'd walked his circle, as the years had turned into decades, he'd lost half his toes, his right ear, and his left thumb and index finger to frostbite. He lifted his feet in the moonlight and wiggled what was left of his toes, the dark spots like missing teeth.

He could still walk; his hearing hadn't faltered; he was right-handed. He never complained.

He didn't have to go back to Elizabeth every autumn for apple seeds anymore, either. Another powerful blessing. His apple orchards stretched all along the northern banks of the Ohio Valley, from Steubenville, Ohio, to Cairo, Illinois. A thousand river miles of apple trees! Where there were apples, there were seeds.

His apple trees grew in every county in Ohio, most of Indiana, and downstate Illinois. His apple trees thrived in Iowa along the western bank of the Mississippi River. Pioneers took his apple seedlings north into Michigan, farther northwest into the Wisconsin Territory, and farther south into Tennessee, Missouri, and Arkansas. More apples for more neighbors.

He could walk into any town and the folks would besiege him with offers.

"Sup with us tonight. We have the finest roast beef in town."

"Speak at my garden club, Johnny. I've already told them you'd be attending."

"Do speak at my ladies' reading circle, Mr. Chapman. Our husbands have forbade us to read *The Last of the Mohicans,* claiming it's not suitable reading for ladies. Of course, we've all read it anyway, and since you know the Indians—"

"I'm a reporter for the *Illinois State Register* newspaper, and—"

"Johnny, I'm going to give you this rifle. I was going to send it to my son—he's in Buffalo Bayou, along the San Jacinto River, fighting for Texas independence. You need this rifle more than he does. He's got the army to protect him."

"Johnny, you should run for president."

"Our whole town has been saving seeds for Johnny Appleseed. Oh, you can't carry ten bags full? When can you come back for the rest?"

"Johnny, I'm going to give you this dog. Her dam is the best hunting dog I've got. You need a companion in the wilderness."

"Johnny, your apples are the best in creation for making applejack. Most of last year's harvest is in brown jugs in the woodshed. You're welcome to drink as much as you want and to carry away as much as you'd care to."

Most of the time he had to say no, especially when it came to the roast beef and rifles. And the applejack. It was hard, explaining to folks about his mission and the need to travel light.

The hardest part was explaining what their kindness meant to him. The sun, the rain, and the apple seed—and these good folks. His life was an ark of loaves and fishes, four-thousand-fold.

🌳🌳🌳

He decided to go to Elizabeth, Pennsylvania, one last time. Perhaps Mrs. Elizabeth Van Kirk was still alive. She would appreciate seeing her mother's Bible again. It would be a comfort to swap stories about her sister, Esther Bushnell.

He'd also heard that Cornplanter was still alive. That surely couldn't be true. Still, he'd like to visit the Seneca again and see their apple trees.

East of Cincinnati, he was astonished at all the people. Farms, towns, and cities had sprung up like mushrooms after a long rain. In between civilization's marks were apple trees, almost as stately as the ones he remembered from his boyhood.

The riverbank wilderness he remembered from the early days of his mission was long gone. Riverfront towns, dockyards, and piers had taken its place. Where once indignant squirrels and chipmunks had chattered at him, dogs now barked.

From shady porches, housecats bristled their tails and flattened their ears as he passed by. They glared at him, their pupils suddenly wide, like fast-moving thunderclouds.

Johnny's hair and beard were white as snow and almost reached his calves. He'd gone so long without cutting either one, it was a matter of curiosity and superstition to him now. How long could they grow? Could they sweep to his feet someday? He reckoned himself to be another Samson, his strength in his hair.

He'd lost so many toes to frostbite that he had to stuff newspapers in his boots for strength and balance. Even so, he walked with a peculiar rolling gait, like someone standing in a rowboat for the first time.

In the warm months, he wore a burlap coffee sack that draped below his knees. And nothing else, save an old piece of rope tied around his middle to keep his Bible in place.

If I were a housecat, I'd glare at me, too, I reckon.

Just outside Marietta, Johnny saw two housewives on ladders, picking apples from a stand of trees.

"Those are McIntosh, aren't they?" he called out. "And Ashram's Kernel?"

The ladies looked down on him, clutching at their skirts and trying to balance their apple baskets against their waists.

124

"These are wild apple trees," the first one said. "No one owns them."

"Right you are," Johnny replied. "These trees are more than thirty-five years old. It does my heart good to see the fruits of my labor."

"Nobody owns these trees," the second housewife called out. "They're wild trees."

"Apple trees don't start wild, ma'am. Somebody always has to plant them. I planted these trees for you and your family."

"Land sakes!" The first housewife dropped her basket of apples. The apples commenced to roll toward the riverbank. He scooped one up and bit into it. It was an Ashram's Kernel all right—the skin the same dull color of wood, the firm, crunchy flesh more tangy than sweet.

"You're Johnny Appleseed, aren't you!" the first housewife shouted. "Alma, this is Johnny Appleseed! *You* planted this orchard! All my life we've speculated as to who planted these trees. Every winter of my life we've had apples. Every winter of my life."

"I'm right pleased to hear it."

She scurried down the ladder. As she talked, Johnny helped her pick up her apples. "Johnny Appleseed! As I live and breathe! You have to come home with me. It's Mr. Chapman, isn't it? I'll give you the best supper you've ever eaten. Catfish, pork chops, pot greens, cornbread, blackberry cobbler, apple pie, buttermilk, and store-bought tea."

"The cornbread, pot greens, blackberry cobbler, pie, and tea would be a powerful blessing, ma'am. What's your name?"

"I'm Mrs. Lovinia Van Swearingen. Johnny Appleseed! Land sakes! You're more famous than . . . than Sir Walter Scott!"

🌳🌳🌳

After supper, Johnny dozed before the fire in a rocking chair. He awoke with a start: The two Van Swearingen children were tugging at his elbows.

"We told Mama," the little boy announced, "we wouldn't go to sleep unless you told us a story. We already told Mama."

"A story? Well, now. Let me think." Johnny shook his head hard to clear the cobwebs.

Mrs. Van Swearingen called from the sink, "Samuel, Mr. Chapman is worn out after his long journey. Let him sleep in peace."

"It's all right, Mrs. Van Swearingen. How old are you, Samuel?"

"Six. Molly's four."

"I know an Indian story. Would the two of you like to hear that?"

"Indians!" Samuel Van Swearingen's eyes were huge. "My great-granddaddy used to fight the Indians."

"I used to live with Indians. Well, I used to visit with them. Just as I'm visiting with you now."

Samuel looked Johnny straight in the eye. "I wouldn't have been scared."

"I wasn't scared either. They're good friends of mine."

"The Indians are friends?" Molly whispered.

"Molly's scared of Indians," Samuel announced.

Johnny turned to her. "Are you afraid of Indians, Molly?"

She gave him a solemn nod.

"That's too bad."

Samuel pointed to Johnny's left hand. "Did the Indians do that? Chop off your thumb and finger?"

"Samuel!" Mrs. Van Swearingen shouted from the sink. "Don't be rude! And don't scare your sister!"

"Let me ask you something, Samuel," Johnny replied. "Would a friend do that to you?"

"No."

"My friends the Seneca didn't do this to me. This is a story about Fox and Wolf."

Samuel and Molly sat down on the rug and turned their faces up to listen.

"Wolf was smart, but Fox was smarter. They lived in Seneca country, a land of deep snow and long, cold winters.

"Fox and Wolf would nod to each other as they

chased the same rabbits, squirrels, moles, and mice over the game trails. Fox and Wolf stayed out of each other's way. They were good neighbors. They were not good friends.

"One winter was especially cold. The snow-laden wind beat against the tree trunks and set the branches to shivering. It charged down the animal burrows like a starving wolverine after a mouse."

Samuel and Molly's shoulders shivered in sympathy. Molly tucked her hands into her sleeves for warmth.

"As the days grew colder," Johnny continued, "the sun pulled his night blanket closer around himself. That made the days shorter as well.

"For Fox and Wolf, life was hard. Their food slept deep within the earth, huddled in fur-lined rabbit burrows or snug in mole or mouse holes. Even the squirrels stayed in the tree hollows.

"Fox and Wolf were so cold and hungry! The cold wind made their eyes smart and their noses and bellies ache.

"On the coldest, darkest day, Fox saw a Seneca warrior trudging through the forest pulling a sled behind him. On the sled were two strings of plump, tasty fish.

"Fox's mouth began to water. Fish were his favorite, and they were so hard to catch! Especially in winter, when every lake, every river, every stream lay sleeping, covered with a thick blanket of ice and snow.

"'I know how to get those fish,' Fox said to himself, 'every last tasty one of them.'

"He ran ahead of the Seneca warrior and found a tree in the man's path. Fox lay down on the tree's roots just as the warrior was upon him.

"'Brother!' he wailed. 'I've broken my leg! Help me!'

"The warrior stopped and took a good, long look at Fox.

"'A broken leg, you say? A fox with a broken leg makes a better fur hat than a fox. I'm taking you home.'"

"Mama's got a fox-skin hat," Samuel announced.

"Samuel, don't interrupt," Mrs. Van Swearingen said.

"Well, Fox whimpered and cried as the warrior placed him on the sled," Johnny continued. "The man pushed off for home, his snowshoes squeaking like a mouse on the feather-light snow.

"Fox waited for the best moment to escape. He took one string of fish in his mouth and took off running!

"'Ho! Ho!' he laughed. 'Nothing tastes better than a string of fish on a cold day! Goodbye, brother!'

"The Seneca warrior shook his fist at Fox. 'Someday,' he shouted, his voice dying away as Fox ran farther and farther into the forest, 'someday I'll get my fur hat.'

"Fox laughed. With great relish and pleasure he began to eat his fish.

"Soon Wolf came up.

"Wolf's mouth began to water when he saw Fox's fish.

"'Brother,' Wolf said, 'a fish shared with friends tastes better than a fish eaten alone.'

"'That's true,' Fox replied as he gulped down his last fish. 'But my fish are gone. I can show you how to get some of your own.'

"Soon, Wolf lay against a tree trunk, howling and crying. 'My leg!' he moaned. 'I've broken my leg! Somebody help me!'

"The Seneca warrior rushed through the forest toward Wolf, his second string of plump fish bumping behind him on the sled.

"'I've been tricked once today,' he shouted angrily. 'I won't be fooled again.'

"Wolf took off running, but the warrior was quick. He caught Wolf and knelt to tie him up with a strong grapevine rope.

"'A wolf with a broken leg makes a better fur hat than a wolf,' he said. 'And I'll have enough of you left over for a blanket.'

"At that moment, Fox ran out from behind a tree and grabbed the second string of fish. Glancing behind him, he laughed as the Seneca warrior jumped up and down in anger. Wolf shot off in the opposite direction, with his head down and his tail between his legs.

"Fox ran and ran. Soon he was safe within the forest. He rolled on his belly, laughing and laughing. 'No fish, no fur hat, and no fur blanket today,' he shouted. 'And more fish for me!'"

Molly and Samuel giggled and giggled. "Tell us another!" Samuel shouted.

"Another!" Molly chimed in.

"No more stories," Mrs. Van Swearingen said. "Off to bed."

"Good night," Johnny said. He waved as Mrs. Van Swearingen nudged her children up the stairs.

He must have fallen asleep again, for this time it was Mrs. Van Swearingen tugging at his elbow.

"Mr. Chapman, we have a guest room. May I help you upstairs?"

"I don't need help."

But he did need help. His legs were as wobbly as a spring lamb's. She grasped him firmly by the elbow and helped him up the stairs.

"My husband's father lived here with us until the end," she said. "I know how to take care of an elderly gentleman."

An elderly gentleman? She can't mean me!

"Sleep as long as you like tomorrow, Mr. Chapman. Breakfast anytime. I can't believe it. Johnny Appleseed—in my house!"

It wasn't so long ago that Johnny could sleep as soundly as a baby and in all weathers. Now he slept in the fits and starts of an old man. But that night he was so tired and the bed was so luxurious, he slept until long after daybreak.

THE OLD STATES
1836

A week later, Mr. and Mrs. Van Swearingen walked Johnny down to the docks and put him on a steamboat called the *New Orleans.* They insisted on paying for a first-class ticket, three days upriver to Pittsburgh.

"I walk more than one thousand miles in a given year," Johnny protested. "I've walked to Pittsburgh more than twenty times."

"Our treat," Mr. Van Swearingen said firmly.

"Get some rest," Mrs. Van Swearingen said, firmer still.

Johnny had his own cabin, his own bed, his own table, and his own chairs. The *New Orleans* also provided plates, silverware, and three hot meals a day.

He took a nap on the bed after the nooning. Afterward, he went up on deck to take the air.

When he returned to his cabin below decks, he was surprised. The remains of his meal had been taken back to the galley. The bed was made up, fresh with clean linens.

The luxury and attention made him skittish and unsettled.

He took to spending more and more time sitting on a bench on the main deck in the open air. The *New Orleans* was painted all in white, three layers high, with so much filigree and fancy latticework, it looked like a wedding cake. On the top layer were two black pipes the size of forty-year-old oak trees. From them, the smoke and steam poured forth, swept to the stern by the stiff breeze. Sometimes droplets landed, still warm, on his bare arms.

Johnny liked to sit astern and watch the paddlewheel go round and round. It was hypnotic: the paddlewheel, the water tumbling from the paddles like a waterfall, the unceasing circle—his mind drifted to the early days of his mission.

In those days, he had paddled his double canoe down a vacant and quiet Ohio, with just the animals and birds to keep him company.

Foraging critters used to worry the cornmeal sack and apple seed pouches. Deer families would drink from the river. When the canoes slipped by, they'd look up in alarm, their muzzles dripping water, their ears quivering.

Now the Ohio was crowded with steamboats, fishing

boats, fur traders on rafts, and pleasure craft. Merchant ships from the South bulged with pine planks, great barrels of turpentine, and cotton and tobacco bales. There were so many river craft, Johnny reckoned he could walk from one riverbank to the other without getting his feet wet.

On the second day, a hearty cheer rose up from all decks as a troopship, loaded to the gunwales with soldiers, steamed by. Judging from their singing, those young men were off to Texas, to chase General Antonio López de Santa Anna and his army of thousands back to Mexico.

The men sang:

"Santyanno came that day. Go away, Santyanno.
Santyanno gained that day, along the plains of Mexico.
Mexico! Oh, Mexico! Go away, Santyanno.
Mexico is a place I'll know, along the plains of Mexico."

Johnny sighed: another terrible war. It was the Texans who first took to calling the Mexican general Santyanno, as a way to shore up their courage. All his life there had been wars and bitter skirmishes—with Indians, with the British, with the French-speaking Indians of Canada, the Spanish, and now the Mexicans.

What if he'd sown apple seeds in Texas? Could the bounty of the apple have stopped this war? Could these young men be working their family farms, or learning trades, instead of being crammed together on a troopship, already so far from home?

I reckon not. Cornplanter once told me that my apples had changed everything—everything but the human heart.

And yet, how many battles have my orchards averted? How many times has the apple's bounty deafened wars' alarms? How many times has someone thought: No, I'm satisfied. I've got no need to fight this day? How many times has this everyday miracle occurred?

Thirty-seven years! And how many endless shovelfuls of earth? It makes my shoulders creak just thinking about it. But I've learned to have faith in my mission, to believe in "the evidence of things not seen."

The troopship steamed downriver toward the Mississippi, the singing fainter and fainter, like the fading light on a winter's afternoon:

"Times is hard and the pay is low. Go away, Santyanno.
Time for us to roll and go, along the plains of Mexico.
Mexico! Oh, Mexico! Go away, Santyanno.
Mexico is a place I'll know, on the plains of Mexico."

He watched for broadhorns of the sort he used to build. In the Pittsburgh of his youth, westering pioneers had taken the river roads to their new homes in the borderlands. He saw no broadhorns.

135

He smiled at the mature apple trees. Nothing is prettier than a stand of apple trees, the branches striving toward heaven, the apples tilting toward man.

The *New Orleans* chugged upriver: the Ohio shore, the western Virginia shore, then the Pennsylvania shores.

Johnny was astounded by the noise and energy. Dockside, passengers rushed to disembark even as more passengers scurried forward to board. Stevedores sweated mightily, pushing drums of corn and flour into the hold before the *New Orleans* curved into the river again.

Where were all these folks going in such a hurry? What was the rush? Where had all this hustle and bustle come from? He felt as though he'd been napping below decks for fifteen years!

Out in Iowa, Illinois, and Indiana, the sleepy farms and homesteads, the tiny churches and quiet country cemeteries, had reminded him of his childhood in Longmeadow, Massachusetts.

He would sit on the front porch of a log cabin or sod house with the womenfolk and children. Together they'd watch a long, drowsy summer afternoon ease into twilight. The prairie bees, buzzing lazily from thistle to buttercup to larkspur to black-eyed Susan, sounded like someone snoring in a back bedroom.

He'd read his favorite verses, mostly the Psalms, out

loud to the rhythm of the wife or eldest daughter thumping milk to butter in the churn. Where did all these sects come from all of a sudden? These days there were as many ways to praise His name as there were people on this earth.

Well, the Psalms offended no one. After thirty-seven years, royal David's pages were fingered to transparency.

The younger children chased one another in the yard. As the sun tilted westward and the shadows lengthened, the man of the house would ease his bones onto the porch with a groan after working the fields all day. He'd gulp a cup of water from the rain barrel. Within moments he'd be snoring, his sun hat shielding his face.

The light would soften. Then twilight would fall like a benediction, with the cooling air and the promise of a new day.

Here in the old states, though, this nation seemed ready to burst at the seams.

The passengers hustling on and off the *New Orleans* didn't look like country people, either. He saw no lean men in buckskins and coonskin caps, rifles at the ready. There were no timid women in faded calicoes blushing under sunbonnets. The passengers' children were not dressed in ragged hand-me-downs.

These people wore suits and ties, silks and parasols. They all had shoes. The women had fluffy dogs on their laps, most no bigger'n woodchucks.

Children stared at him. "Mama, look," one shouted. "Is that old man a circus clown? His hair is past his knees! And a burlap sack for a suit!"

"It's not polite to stare," the boy's mother said, staring at Johnny.

"He hasn't got any thumbs!" another boy exclaimed.

Johnny smiled bravely and held up his right thumb. "I've got one thumb. How many do you have?"

"Below decks. Now." The boy's mother pushed him away.

The other passengers averted their eyes.

Johnny kept his gaze on the paddlewheel for the rest of the afternoon.

At the next stop, the stevedores rolled great bales of indigo into the hold. Their sweating hands and arms soaked up the dark blue from the indigo blossoms. The boys on deck took to laughing at the blue-armed stevedores instead of Johnny.

🌳🌳🌳

Pittsburgh was like the very mouth of Hell.

As the *New Orleans* landed, a bell rang out, loud enough to wake the dead, loud enough to make them jump in fright.

On the Allegheny side, hundreds of men streamed out of one huge door of a manufactory, as more men streamed in another door.

There were more manufactories all along the Monongahela side. Another bell rang out, and another. More workers, thousands of them, pushed in and out of manufactories as though they were harried minnows, swimming upstream or down.

Johnny disembarked and wandered down Main Street, mouth agape. Far down the street were more manufactories, surely the size of those cathedrals in the old countries. Except these massive buildings hadn't taken generations to build. None of these manufactories had been here fifteen years before.

The Keystone Iron and Copper Works, the Fort Pitt Foundry, the William Hays Tannery and Harness Works, the North Star Foundry, the Three Rivers Coke Pit, and many others had replaced the twenty-four taverns and public houses from the old days.

Gone, too, were the scruffy lumbermen of the old days. Instead, there were workers, thousands of them and all in a hurry, speaking languages Johnny had never heard before. They pushed him aside, scurrying to their jobs.

The hillsides around the city were dotted with tiny shacks, most no better than the lean-to his father had lived in the last years of his life.

Homes for workers.

Smokestacks poured foul-smelling smoke into the bright sunshine. Every once in a while, great gouts of ash shot out of the stacks and drifted below the smoke, shutting out the noonday sun. Sometimes fire leaped from the smokestacks, scorching the air.

The workers were covered in greasy soot. Soon Johnny was covered, too. He pushed his beard up over his face to shut out the horrific rotten-egg smell from the coke pits.

In between the manufactories were stacks of coal, taller than some Illinois hills. Stacks of cowhides and pigskins crowded the side yards. The skins smelled sickly sweet, like an animal left to rot in the elements. The tanneries themselves filled his nose with the acrid stench of scorched hair, burned hooves, and chemicals.

Wonder of wonders, there were women in those crowds of workers! Women in shirts and trousers! Women working in manufactories! Women smelting iron ore and tanning hides! Women buying drinks in the taverns after working like men all day! Women . . . belly up to the bar!

Within minutes, the streets were empty. A slow pounding of metal against metal arose from within the Pittsburgh Iron & Copper Foundry Works.

Johnny felt the pounding in his bones, in his very teeth. He covered his ears. Were they all deaf, these poor souls?

Workers squatted on the riverbank to wash their hands. A slick of grease and oil glimmered on top of the water like a rainbow. It was the first pretty thing Johnny had seen since landing.

The workers' wrists had a scrim of oily soot around them as they wiped their hands on their shirts. No one was drinking the river water. They ran into back-alley taverns to slake their thirst instead.

It was at that moment that an iron horse chugged across Main Street. Johnny had heard tales, but he'd never seen one up close. The iron horse screamed to a stop.

Steam. It was a Scotsman, he'd heard, a man named Watt, who'd figured out that the same steam that whistles out of a teakettle could power a ship or a train. Or turn iron ore into more railroad tracks for more iron horses. Or work a machine that could turn cowhides into boots, saddlebags, and buggy whips.

The engine pulled ten cars behind her. This was where the coal and the hides had come from! The cars were overflowing with materials for the manufactories. At the very back of the train were people.

"The westering pioneers!" Johnny exclaimed. "They travel by train now."

The pioneers' weary faces were soot black; only their pale eyes shone through.

What happened to my spring? The spring I used to drink from?

Johnny remembered the location, but there was a

manufactory upon it now. How could a spring stop flowing? Where upon the earth, or within the earth, could the water go?

Despite a powerful thirst, he didn't dare drink the river water.

"Elizabeth. The orchards in Elizabeth will be a tonic. I'll sleep on the banks of the Monongahela tonight. I'll have plenty of time for a visit with the Van Kirks tomorrow."

A Circle Breaks
1836

Thirty-seven autumns before, Johnny had ridden Clabber down the eastern banks of the Monongahela River on his way to Mr. William Van Kirk's cider press.

He remembered the red maple leaves, the color of Rome apples, pattering softly into the clear, rushing water. In the shallows minnows swam.

Now the Monongahela River was a sort of milky brown. The water lapped soapsuds against slimy river rocks devoid of turtles. There couldn't be fish living in that water?

Dead trees haunted both sides of the embankment.

What was wrong with these trees? Not even bark surrounded the bleached trunks, not even birds perched on branches as white as exposed bone.

Johnny slept uneasily that warm night, in a world that seemed as dead as a night in January. Even the insects were missing.

By the time he got to Elizabeth the next morning, the river was cleaner. The trees here were leafed out in autumn color—glorious shades of red, orange, yellow, and plum. Birds sashayed from branch to branch. Chipmunk and squirrel chatter delighted his ears.

It was quiet and peaceful. Finally, water safe to drink again, and bathe in again! He found a rock pool and drank and drank.

The familiar tang of applejack and cider drifted like clouds through the golden October air. The cider presses were still in operation. Elizabeth hadn't changed at all!

The joy and relief brought tears to his eyes.

"I'm looking for the Van Kirks," Johnny said to an orchard man.

"The Van Kirks? Yah, yah." The man pointed to a grand brick house on a far hill. "In dere you find 'em."

"Thank you, sir."

🌳🌳🌳

The Van Kirks live here?

The Van Kirks' new house was south of the orchards. Even from a thousand yards away, it looked as large as one of Pittsburgh's manufactories. Two stories, maybe three; bricks by the thousands. A carriage drive wound down the hill, flanked on both sides by rhododendron bushes.

Turrets poked into the sky from all four corners. To the left was a carriage house, as big as an Indiana farmhouse. An iron filigree fence ran along the property as far as Johnny could see.

Gracing the front lawn were apple trees, the biggest he'd seen since his boyhood in Massachusetts. The old trees did his heart good, although he had to wonder how one-hundred-year-old apple trees could be growing in Elizabeth, Pennsylvania.

Johnny gave the front door a soft knock. After a long wait, it was opened by a man dressed in a shad-belly coat with tails, breeches, and black boots to the knee. He had powdered hair, clubbed in a black ribbon. He looked like George Washington.

They both were startled. The man who looked like George Washington recovered first. "May I be of service, sir?"

"I'm looking for the Van Kirks—William and Elizabeth—or their son, Willie. I'm a friend from the old days."

"Indeed. I regret to inform you that Mr. Van Kirk is deceased. It is Madame's custom to retire upstairs after luncheon. She will descend for afternoon tea presently. May I tell the mayor who is calling?"

Johnny knew the man was speaking English, but he had to repeat the sentences in his mind a few times before they sank in.

"I'm—I'm John Chapman. They know me as Johnny Appleseed. The mayor? Willie's the *mayor?*"

"Indeed. If you would wait in the drawing room, sir."

The man was halfway down the hall when he stopped. "If you could walk this way, Mr. . . . Mr. Appleseed?"

"Chapman."

"Mr. Chapman. Very good, sir."

The house unfolded around him. With each step, Johnny's bare feet sank into deep rugs as soft as honey. Each room they passed had a separate color scheme, as though each room were a separate house.

The man who looked like George Washington left him in a cozy room with a small but well-tended fire. Johnny sat down gratefully in a rocker in front of the fire. His eyes felt weighted, heavy.

He awoke to the man who looked like George Washington giving his throat a mighty clearing.

Willie Van Kirk stood to the side.

"Sir? Are you Johnny Appleseed?"

"Willie?" he murmured. "Is that you? Home from Yale College?"

"I'm him, all right," Willie Van Kirk said cheerfully. "Some tea, Beech. And tell my mother Johnny Appleseed is here."

"Very good, sir."

Willie pulled a chair up to the fire. "Johnny Appleseed! My mother will be so pleased to see you. When did you last visit us—fifteen, twenty years ago?"

"It's been fifteen years. You look just like your father did when I first met him. I'm sorry for your loss, Willie. Your father was a good man."

"Thank you, Johnny. He talked about you all the time."

"Who was that man dressed as George Washington?"

Willie laughed. "That was Beech, a real dyed-in-the-wool English butler. How about that?"

"What does a butler do?" Johnny muttered, still half asleep.

"I can't rightly say. He's busy all day, though, I can tell you that."

Johnny asked, "You're the mayor? Of Pittsburgh?"

"Oh, no, just Elizabeth. My law practice is in Pittsburgh. I'm also a representative for the Commonwealth of Pennsylvania. I've just returned from Harrisburg."

Johnny looked blank.

"Our state's capital. You know, government?"

"Oh. . . . I came here to see your folks, Willie, to reminisce about the old days."

The mayor nodded. "My father died about ten years ago, just as I was building this house."

"He was a good man," Johnny repeated. "So this is a new house? But it looks so old. How can there be hundred-year-old apple trees outside?"

Willie tapped the side of his nose. "The trick is not

to make the house *look* new. Those trees were brought here, all the way from Philadelphia."

"But one hundred years ago this land belonged to the Susquehannocks. They didn't have apple trees."

The mayor raised one corner of his mouth in a smile. "How have you been, Johnny?"

"Elizabeth is a sight for sore eyes. It hasn't changed a bit."

"Oh, I have big plans for Elizabeth." The mayor winked and pulled his chair closer. "I know you can keep a secret. I intend to bid on a foundry. A gentleman back in Allentown wants a paint and glassworks foundry right here in western Pennsylvania.

"I'll have to work quickly. There's a consortium of businessmen out in Cleveland, Ohio, who'd like that foundry, too."

Johnny reeled back in horror. "No, Willie, you can't do that! Ever since Cincinnati . . . Why, this country's so different! It's so loud! It's so crowded! Everyone's so busy! Do you remember the Ohio Valley the way it used to be? The trees the size of hearths, the clean water and air, the quiet, and all the animals?"

"Progress, Mr. Chapman. Progress and jobs. There's no stopping either one once they get started."

"Let the Ohioans have it. Please, Willie, for your mother's sake. Those poor souls in Pittsburgh—they're like ants. Like, like rats—"

The mayor's mouth was a thin line. "Those ants, as you call them, are from Eastern Europe, from the Austro-Hungarian Empire. Do you have any idea of what it's like living under the Hapsburgs? Under that craven idiot Francis Joseph?

"Why, they were no better than slaves back in Slovenia, Bohemia, Transyl . . . Transylvania." Willie waved his hand impatiently. "They came to America with nothing. Here they can earn good wages. Their children can go to school. They could even be citizens someday."

Willie rubbed his hands together. "There must be thousands of them, eager to leave the Old World, eager to find good-paying work here in the New. Thousands of them."

"Willie, they can't even drink the water downriver! I can't even comprehend such horror! Water has been on this earth since the first day of Creation. 'And the Spirit of God moved upon the face of the waters.'"

Willie laughed. "The Lord would want to move fast upon the face of the Monongahela, I'll give you that. But I'm surprised at you, Johnny. Just because our families have been here since before the Revolution, should we shut the door on everyone else? You would deny them the freedom and opportunity we enjoy? You of all people, with your generous heart! I'm surprised at your attitude."

"You misunderstand me, Willie. Surely when those

poor souls quit the Hapsburgs, they didn't expect ...
You know I've never thought much of Pittsburgh, but
now it looks like a festering wound.

"Why would you bring such misery here? Willie!
The very town your father named after your mother!"

Their glares met and clashed. Beech, holding a tray,
cleared his throat. "Your tea, sir."

"Johnny Appleseed!" Elizabeth Van Kirk hobbled
from behind Beech, her left arm out and welcoming.
She grasped a cane in her right hand.

Johnny tried hard not to stare. His old friend's hair
was no longer the warm brown of a female cardinal's
feathers. It was snow white. Her face was as wrinkled
and thin skinned as a root-cellar apple left over until
August.

"Elizabeth." He hoisted himself to his feet.

"Mother." The mayor stood up and offered his chair.

The men waited until Mrs. Van Kirk slowly eased
herself down before they sat again. Mrs. Van Kirk
propped her cane against her leg. Beech set the tea tray
on a mahogany table beside her.

"Join us for dinner, Johnny," the mayor said stiffly.
"We dine at eight."

"Thank you, Willie. You may go." Mrs. Van Kirk settled more comfortably into the chair. "I'll pour, Beech.
You may leave too."

"Yes, madam."

Mrs. Van Kirk waited until both men were out of the room. She raised her eyebrows at Johnny as though they were conspirators.

"Beech doesn't approve of the way I pour out. He thinks tea belongs in a cup, but everyone knows the first half belongs in the saucer to cool. You should see Beech's face when I slurp from a saucer! It's like he's turned to granite."

She poured out the tea into saucers and handed one to Johnny. They added plenty of sugar and slices of lemon and slurped to their hearts' content.

"Don't pay attention to my son, either. Dinner at eight!" She let loose a sort of half laugh, half snort. "The mister and I were fast asleep by eight and awake before the dawn. We'll have a real backwoods supper, Johnny, in your honor. At five o'clock."

She beamed at her old friend from behind her saucer. "Do have some cake. Cook baked it just this morning."

"Thank you." He bit into a wondrous fruitcake, studded with raisins, dates, figs, cherries, and almonds. He ate another slice, and another.

They drank the second half, out of the teacups this time.

"Your fruitcake will put my modest apples out of business, Elizabeth. I've never tasted anything so delicious."

"Have more. And tell me about Esther. You are the only person left who still remembers my dear sister, Esther."

Johnny swallowed fruitcake and tea before speaking again. "I look at you and I have an inkling of what your sister might have looked like, had she lived to old age. I used to read your mother's Bible to her and James by the hour. The first time I met her, she said neither she nor her husband could read."

Elizabeth half snorted, half laughed again. "Oh, Johnny! Of course Esther could read! James, too. My sister could have been a schoolteacher, had women taught in those days."

Johnny's mouth fell open. "She told me she couldn't read."

"She told you that because she wanted you to stay. That was the hook, you see. It was so hard on her, living out in the wilderness. You look surprised. I've kept her letters, mostly about you. She so enjoyed your company.

"Johnny, I look around at all this luxury, all this splendor, and I can't believe I had a sister killed by the Indians. It's like we don't live in the same country anymore. It's like we're not the same people anymore. Don't you think so, too? I can't believe I've lived this long."

"Nor I," Johnny muttered around a mouthful of fruitcake.

Elizabeth Van Kirk's eyes brimmed with tears. "It was a blessing my sister never had children. They would have been . . . well." She dabbed at her eyes with a froth of lace and linen.

Johnny said, "The prairies recollect the old days for me. I spend most of my time in downstate Illinois and western Indiana now. . . . Elizabeth, have you been to Pittsburgh recently? You must stop Willie from building foundries here. I fear your lovely town will never recover."

"I loathe Pittsburgh: I haven't been there in years. But if I forbid Willie to build foundries, he'll just wait until after I die to build them."

"But—"

"Johnny, do you remember when we were children, how men would hanker to go west? Westering was like a disease. Now the grandsons of those men hanker to build foundries and manufactories. Industry is like a disease, too."

"But you could insist—"

"When my son talks about giving good jobs to poor men, it's impossible to argue with him. I'm sorry, Johnny. I've tried."

🌳🌳🌳

The three of them went into another room for supper at five o'clock. After supper they went into yet another room just to sit.

"Would you care to see the greenhouse, Johnny?" Mrs. Van Kirk asked, after coffee had been served. "We have so many exotic plants in the greenhouse. You would enjoy them. We have violets from Africa, and orchids from Siam. A rubber tree from Brazil. And pineapples! Have you ever seen a pineapple? It's the Dutch who grow them ... in the East Indies."

"I'd like to see such wonders."

After finishing their coffee, they walked into the back gardens and toward the greenhouse. Johnny saw an orange light glowing above Pittsburgh.

"The city is on fire," he wailed. "'Her high gates shall be burned with fire.' Those poor souls!"

Willie spoke to Johnny as if he were a small child. "No, no. Those are the night shifts. The foundries and manufactories run all day and all night, seven days a week. Jobs, Mr. Chapman: freedom and opportunity."

"You would do that?" Johnny said angrily, pointing toward Pittsburgh. "You would destroy your parents' town?"

Willie said, low and bitter, "Soon it'll be my town."

"Willie, you don't mean that!" his mother cried out.

"I have to leave!" Johnny shouted. "I can't stay."

The mayor gave him an angry, baffled stare.

Mrs. Van Kirk pulled on his sleeve. "No, Johnny, please—"

Johnny turned and walked toward the house. He

found the drawing room and picked up his cornmeal sack and apple seed pouches.

I'll head north and sit in Cornplanter's longhouse for a spell.

Cornplanter will understand my grieving rage. Then I'll walk—walk without stopping—clear to the prairies of Illinois.

CAESAR
1840

The youngest of the grandnephews, Nathaniel, leaned against Johnny's knee. "Uncle John, when the winter is over, you're not coming back to Ohio? Not ever again for a very long time?"

"Nathaniel Broom," Johnny's sister scolded. "Were you eavesdropping last night? You were supposed to be asleep."

Johnny looked into Nathaniel's wide-open freckled face. The five-year-old was close to tears.

"It's all right, sister. How is a young one ever going to learn anything if he doesn't spy on his elders? Your grandma and I were just talking last night. That's all."

Johnny's sister's house in Mansfield was the closest thing to a home he had. In the late summer, when the black flies swarmed and the gnats were a constant nuisance, Johnny would think about Persis's house, filled with shouting grandchildren and their high-spirited friends.

Her home was like a cave come winter. It was overflowing with people waiting out the cold.

That afternoon in February, the kettle was on the boil and Persis was passing around slices of her apple pie. Her pies were the best, made with plenty of cinnamon and nutmeg, and eight Northern Spy apples to every two Welton Pie apples. She favored maple syrup over sugar, and just a touch of lemon juice to brighten the taste.

Those who wanted it could have a wedge of cheddar on top. The orange cheese melted on the steaming crust, glowing as softly as a winter sunset.

"I'll come back to Mansfield, Nathaniel," Johnny said. "The reason why I wander so far is because it's becoming harder and harder to find open land for apple orchards. Quarter Sections are tapped out. Homesteading is over in Ohio. Farmers prefer grain and livestock to orchards now. These days Ohio might as well be the New England of my boyhood, what with all the towns and cities.

"There's still plenty of open land in Illinois and Iowa for the westering pioneers, Nathaniel. Or maybe I'll try the Wisconsin Territory. I'll always come back to Mansfield for your grandmother's apple pies."

"The Bushnells from church are thinking about packing up and moving to Nebraska," his sister said. "Good farmland is cheap along the river bottoms."

"The Bushnells?" Johnny felt a clutch at his heart. "I once knew a James and Esther Bushnell. I wonder if your friends are related. It's sad to hear of Bushnells leaving, after James and Esther sacrificed so much."

Nathaniel slipped his hand into Johnny's "What did they sacrifice, Uncle John?"

"A lot of hard work, that's what I mean. Persis, do you need help with the tea?"

That evening someone knocked on the front door, three times. Each knock was louder than the next.

Johnny's brother-in-law let in the county tax assessor. Mr. Clawstraight was dressed all in black, as bespoke a county dignitary. His long black cloak was gray, dusted in downy snowflakes. Standing there in the doorway with his craned neck and rounded shoulders, he looked like a roughly hewn tombstone.

"Mr. Clawstraight, good evening. What can I do for you?" William asked.

"Not you, Mr. Broom. Him." He pointed a bony finger in Johnny's direction. "Mr. Chapman, how much land do you own in Richland County?"

"I planted orchards for the pioneers, Mr. Clawstraight. They claimed those orchards as part of their leaseholds."

Mr. Clawstraight looked at him over his spectacles.

Persis offered pie. "The apples are from an orchard my brother planted near thirty years ago."

"No, thank you, Mrs. Broom. You planted this orchard thirty years ago, Mr. Chapman? Indeed. And you don't own this particular orchard?"

"No. It's just behind the Brooms' house. I agree with the Indians' argument. No one really owns land, Mr. Clawstraight. The earth and the fullness thereof belong to God.

"Do we own the sun? The stars? The water? No, we don't, sir. Even the apples in the pie we're eating don't really belong to my sister. We're only strangers passing through, as was the stranger on the road to Jericho.

"Everything on this earth is a blessing, a gift. We can only marvel in gratitude and share these blessings with one another before we go home to our reward."

Mr. Clawstraight took off his glasses and painstakingly polished them.

They all just sat there, watching. What did he want? Why was he here? There was something about him polishing his glasses—so cold and purposeful—just like a cat preening its whiskers in front of a clutch of huddled, uneasy mice.

"Mr. Chapman, you've got apple orchards all over Ohio. Are you saying you don't own them?"

"I have a mission, Mr. Clawstraight. The orchards belong to God. We're to share the apples with one another. The more we share, the more we have to share. Try some of my sister's pie. It's the best in Mansfield."

"I repeat—no, thank you."

"At least sit down by the fire."

Mr. Clawstraight walked over to the fire but stood before it. His cloak steamed; water dripped onto the hearthstones. "I shan't be long. Mr. Chapman, are you familiar with leaseholds?"

"I am."

"Suppose you went into the wilderness and held twenty acres as your own. You cut down the trees, built a cabin, raised crops, raised a family, raised livestock. That would be your farm, wouldn't it? You'd be holding the lease, wouldn't you, Mr. Chapman?"

"Well, again, we're just passing through to our eternal reward and—"

"Mr. Chapman," he said severely. "If someone asked you, 'Where do you live?' you'd say, 'My farm is over there.' Wouldn't you?"

Persis looked at Johnny in alarm. His brother-in-law William shook his head vigorously as a warning.

A warning against what? I haven't an enemy in this world.

"But I don't own a farm. And the orchards belong to God. I don't live anywhere, Mr. Clawstraight." Johnny threw his arms out. "I live everywhere."

Mr. Clawstraight put his glasses back on.

"But according to the law you do own orchards, Mr. Chapman: thousands of them across this state. You're

160

holding thousands of acres in leaseholds under Ohio law." What he said seemed to clutch at Johnny's throat, squeezing. It was hard to breathe. "How long have you been planting orchards? Going on forty years now? Am I correct?"

"Forty-one."

"Johnny!" William shouted.

"Forty-one years," Mr. Clawstraight continued. "That's a lot of held land. Yet most counties show no record of your paying any taxes on that land. Forty-one years of back taxes, with penalties. You owe the state of Ohio thousands upon thousands of dollars in taxes, do you not?"

"'One generation passeth and another generation cometh, but the earth abideth.' The Indians would agree, Mr. Clawstraight."

The tax assessor's smile was as cold as the February night. He wagged his finger at Johnny. "Oh, I can quote the Bible, too, Mr. Chapman. Matthew 22:21: 'Render therefore unto Caesar the things which are Caesar's; and unto God the things which are God's.'

"That's a favorite verse among tax collectors, and for good reason. You haven't rendered therefore unto Caesar, have you, sir?"

"He isn't holding any land," Persis insisted. "He planted those orchards so pioneer families could have apples. If they had an orchard just waiting for them when they arrived, they wouldn't feel homesick for the farms they left behind in Connecticut and Massachusetts."

Johnny's heart was pounding. The tax assessor's clear blue eyes seemed to bore right into him like icicles.

Mr. Clawstraight said, "There is a second matter as well. I have taken the liberty of bringing with me some Quarter Section deeds you've written out, just within this county alone."

He spread the sheets of paper on the sideboard. There were twenty sheets at least, so many that some slipped to the floor.

"Here's one." Mr. Clawstraight lifted a sheet and began to read.

"'I, John Chapman, by occupation a gatherer and planter of apple seeds, hereby enter into agreement with Mr. Winn Winship on this day of August 8th, 1829, the S.W. Quarter Section 20, Township 20, Range 16, Richland County, Homestead Lease for 160 acres. Registrar to the Land Office, to Moses Modie: recorded this day of August 8th, 1829, in Volume 11, Page 483, Richland County Deed Records.'

"And another: 'I, John Chapman, by occupation a gatherer and planter of apple seeds, hereby enter into agreement with Amos Hofsteddler, on this day of November 21st, 1832, the N.W. Quarter Section 15,

Township 20, Range 20, Richland County, Homestead Lease for 120 acres. Registrar to the Land Office, to Orlando Yoder: recorded this day of November 21st, 1832, in Volume 11a, Page 26, Richland County Deed Records.'

"That's two hundred eighty acres alone, Mr. Chapman. And, as you said, not one penny of taxes paid. Shall I read more?"

Johnny picked up a sheet of paper. "These are Richland County Quarter Sections. I've tried to keep up my taxes here. I have Quarter Sections all over the state."

"Johnny!" William warned.

"Are you aware, Mr. Chapman, that there is a tax on the buying and selling of land in Ohio?"

"Captain Welton once warned me of it," he whispered, "before the War of 1812. Taxes—I hadn't thought of that. I don't like taking money for apple trees. They're a blessing from God. What money I do receive, I give to the poor."

Mr. Clawstraight's words squeezed harder. "Again, the state of Ohio has the right to collect taxes on land transactions. The claiming, buying, and transferring of land are taxable endeavors. You weren't aware of that?"

"Don't say another word, Johnny!" William shouted.

"I'm sorry—"

"Johnny!" William stepped forward. He lifted the tax assessor off his feet, opened the front door, and tossed him into the snowy night.

"We'll see you in court, Mr. Chapman!" Mr.

Clawstraight shouted. He scrambled to his feet as William slammed the door.

"They won't bother you, Johnny. They wouldn't dare!" Persis said. Her dark eyes glowed like coals. "You have so many friends. They'll stick up for you."

"They all enjoy the apples."

They looked at one another. Nathaniel spoke up. "Are you leaving Ohio, Uncle John?"

"I don't know," Johnny replied. "I'd say my leaving Ohio is in God's hands."

🌳🌳🌳

The next morning, Mr. Clawstraight was back, this time with Oskar Bernberger, the county bailiff—a huge, glaring man with eyebrows as menacing, bushy, and abundant as two porcupine tails. His forearms were the size of country hams.

"Good day to you, Mr. Chapman. I am here to give you your court summons."

Mr. Clawstraight gave Johnny a sheaf of documents, all tied up in black ribbon.

On the top page was written:

The State of Ohio, on behalf of all counties within the State of Ohio,

vs.

John Nathaniel Chapman,
a citizen of this state and a taxpayer

Plaintiff: For non-payment for taxes, forty-one years in arrears.

Let it be known: John Chapman, by occupation a gatherer and planter of apple seeds, is hereby charged with tax evasion in the claiming, buying, and selling of land in the State of Ohio. . . .

William grabbed the documents and quickly looked them over. He gasped. "They want twenty thousand dollars in back taxes from you, Johnny!"

"Twenty thousand!" Johnny's sister burst into tears. *Twenty thousand dollars.*

Her words hung in the air above her sobs.

Johnny hadn't hired out his labor for money in forty years, not since he'd worked for Mr. Joshua Stadden back in Pittsburgh. In those days, Mr. Stadden paid his carpenters in Spanish coin dollars cut into pieces of eight.

"I scarcely know what American money looks like," Johnny said in a dazed voice. "I've paid the homesteaders for my Quarter Sections with nursery trees. Good folks give me cornmeal, clothes, and boots as I need them. I've never wanted for anything."

Except twenty thousand dollars.

"Mr. Chapman," Mr. Clawstraight said, "have you the twenty thousand dollars to pay for your tax assessment?"

"It might as well be twenty million dollars, Mr. Clawstraight. It might as well be two hundred million."

"Then it is my duty to take you to the county jail. Judge Wexbury will hear your arguments. You will be arraigned tomorrow. Do you know what an arraignment is, Mr. Chapman? You'll be charged tomorrow. Do you have a lawyer?"

"The sun, the rain, and the apple seed. That's all I've ever needed."

Mr. Clawstraight looked at Johnny again over his spectacles.

William stepped forward. "How long will you keep him?"

"Judge Wexbury will charge him tomorrow, before he leaves. He's a circuit judge. We'll have to wait for him to return for the trial."

"When will Judge Wexbury return?" Persis asked.

"October."

"You can't keep Johnny until October!" William cried.

Mr. Clawstraight leaned his head back and fastened his gaze on Johnny. "Indeed we must, Mr. Broom," he replied. "This is Johnny Appleseed. He could be halfway to Iowa by the March thaw."

14

Four-Thousand-Fold
1840

"'In the day of prosperity be joyful, but in the day of adversity consider: God also hath set the one over against the other, to the end that man should find nothing that will be after him.'

"Well, I didn't have to find out about prison," Johnny said. "I could have imagined it just as easily."

His own father, dead these twenty years, had spent time in the army's prison for drunken and disorderly conduct.

"We have something in common now, my father and I. That's something of a blessing, I reckon. Don't you think so, Mr. Pfefferkopf?"

His cell was ten paces in one direction, seven paces going the other. His cellmate, a swarthy man named Pfefferkopf, didn't answer, just eyed him wolfishly, as was his habit.

But not for long. One morning the bailiff took him

away. Pfefferkopf never returned, and Johnny actually missed him.

The one window looked out onto the prison yard. Within the yard grew a mature buckeye tree. Johnny took to watching it as a surrogate for the return of spring: bare branches, then buds, and then thousands of fluffy white blossoms with feathery centers.

May, then, and the yearly miracle of spring.

For the first time in forty-two springs, he could not plant apple seeds. His apple seed pouches lay folded and empty in his sister's pantry.

This was worse punishment than anything Mr. Clawstraight or Judge Wexbury could do to him. The warm air, scented with apple blossoms, drifted through the prison-cell window and filled his heart with such longing and impatience, it felt ready to burst.

He watched the sun wheel across the sky by day and the stars slowly shift places by night. After spending most of his life in the out-of-doors, Johnny could tell the season, the month, sometimes even the date, just by the position of the stars.

🌳🌳🌳

William and Persis told him he could be facing fifteen years in prison. They stood in the corridor and talked to Johnny through the bars of his prison cell.

"I won't live that long," Johnny replied. "I'm sixty-six years old come September."

"For that be grateful," William said. "Johnny, of the two charges, the leasehold tax is the weakest. They can't prove you planted all those orchards, what with Captain Elijah Welton out there planting apple seeds, too. Furthermore, plenty of pioneers planted nursery trees they brought with them from back East. It would be impossible to know who planted what and when."

William grabbed hold of the prison bars and gave them a good yank. They didn't budge. "It's those Quarter Sections; everything is written out, signed, notarized, and filed in dozens of courthouses around the state. You're paid up in Richland County, but you're delinquent everywhere else.

"I've sent word out on the coach roads for Captain Welton to speak in your defense. He might show up. There are the canals, too, now. Barge captains are spreading the word that you need help."

"Thank you for everything, William."

"You must be terrified, Johnny," Persis exclaimed. She gave him a covered pot of hot water. A sliver of soap and a towel perched on top.

"I'm not, sister," he replied easily. "Nothing scares me anymore. I've learned that a wall is just a wall."

She stared at him blankly.

"Those blue-faced Scots scaled my wall long since. We're neighbors now. The Glory of Rome! In prison!" Johnny laughed merrily. "They can only take from me what I'm willing to give."

Persis started to cry.

William said in a low voice, "Johnny, don't talk nonsense. They'll take you right out of prison and land you in the lunatic asylum in Columbus."

"You're right," Johnny said cheerfully. "Do you remember my spirit-wives, Esther and Elizabeth?"

William's eyes were hooded, wary. "I remember you speaking of them."

"Earthly friends have crowded them out of my life, I reckon. They've been patient: They've called on me again as the weeks in prison slowly transform into months."

"October," William said bitterly. Persis cried harder.

"Most of the time I sleep," Johnny replied with a smile. "For that I'm grateful. These tired old bones need the rest. When this is over, I'm going to the Wisconsin Territory. The Boston Belle should thrive up there around Fort Snelling. That variety needs a cold winter."

William gave the prison bars another yank. "You and your apples."

🌳🌳🌳

On a cold morning late in October, Bailiff Bernberger came to fetch Johnny. He unlocked Johnny's cell with a key; the door creaked open.

"Judge Wexbury wants to see you in his chambers."

"Very well, Mr. Bernberger. How are the wife and children? Has Mrs. Bernberger had her baby yet?"

The Bailiff beamed from under his porcupine eyebrows. "She has: another healthy girl, Mr. Chapman."

"That's wonderful news. Give her my best."

"That I will. She worries about you."

"Please tell Mrs. Bernberger how much I enjoyed Sunday's apples-and-cabbage slaw. It's the apple cider vinegar and sugar that gives it the sweet-sour taste, isn't it? I believe I tasted caraway, too."

"I know nothing of cookery, Mr. Chapman. I'll tell her you enjoyed it."

They went down the hall and up the stairs to a large room. Judge Wexbury sat behind a large desk. There were plenty of chairs.

Johnny stood open-mouthed in astonishment. In each chair sat someone he knew! More friends stood along the back of the room. All of them were nodding and smiling encouragingly.

Judge Wexbury looked down his long nose at Johnny. "It appears you have some friends who'd like to speak on your behalf, Mr. Chapman."

"Yes, Your Honor."

"Most of these people have already given their testimony to the county clerk. Some have insisted that they speak aloud."

Persis Broom jumped up. "I insist, Your Honor."

The judge sighed. "Your name for the record?"

"Persis Broom."

"Your relationship with the defendant?"

"He's my brother."

"Tell us about your brother, Mrs. Broom."

"Well. My brother is the happiest person I know precisely because he doesn't own anything. He's never had to worry about losing the farm or the house, because he's never owned a farm or a house. He's never learned to distrust, because no one has ever tried to steal from him or cheat him. What could they steal? He owns nothing. How could they cheat him? He wants for nothing.

"No one hates him because he is the envy of no one.

"Everything he owns he's wearing. And if someone needed his saucepan or his Bible, or his coffee-sack tunic, he'd joyfully give them away and call it a blessing: a chance to be generous.

"He eats nothing but fruit and vegetables. He doesn't believe in killing for food. He won't eat pie crust because of the lard; he'll scoop the apple filling right out of it and only eat that. He won't light a candle in case beef tallow was mixed in with the wax.

"Oh, my brother's peculiar, and I don't pretend to understand him. It's as though he doesn't live among us. It's as though he walks three feet off the ground.

"He lives his life for others. He treats everyone and

everything with compassion and loving-kindness. And he's so happy! Happy all the time!" She sat down and wiped her eyes with a handkerchief.

"Thank you, Mrs. Broom," Judge Wexbury said. "Mr. Thomas Stadden?" A man came forward.

"Thomas?" Johnny asked, his eyes wide.

The man grinned back. "It's me, Johnny."

"And how do you know the defendant, Mr. Stadden?"

"Your Honor, Mr. Chapman used to come by our homestead when I was a boy. He used to work for my uncle, Mr. Joshua Stadden, in Pittsburgh. That's how we came to know him, through my uncle."

"What do you remember about Mr. Chapman?"

Thomas smiled. "He was the kindest man I'd ever met. He used to borrow my father's whittling knife and make me bears, raccoons, and horses out of wood. He made my sister, Helen, an entire doll family. She never married. Helen gave the doll family to my daughter, who in turn will give it to my granddaughters someday.

"He told us a story once about a bear family. One winter when he was real sick, he found a hollow log. He was going to spend the night in the log, but when he climbed in, he felt bear fur against his hands.

"He told me he shot out of that log like a ball out of a cannon."

Judge Wexbury looked down his nose at Thomas. "And why is this story important?"

"Johnny Appleseed let them lie! He let the sow and her cubs sleep. Anyone else would've shot the bears and dragged them into the snow. Anyone else would've jumped into the log to enjoy the warmth the bears had left behind. Anyone else would've roasted the bear meat for breakfast and sold their skins and the rendered fat for a pretty penny. Not him."

"Thank you, Mr. Stadden."

🌳🌳🌳

"Your name for the record?"

Another man settled into the witness box. "My name is Noah Zane, Your Honor."

Noah Zane! A grown man! Where has the time gone?

Judge Wexbury asked, "And how do you know the defendant?"

"He used to visit us in Zanesville at my grandfather's place." Mr. Zane laughed. "My grandfather was Ebenezer Zane, and he dearly loved to talk about the old days. He could spend hours telling stories about his life as a pioneer and Indian fighter.

"We Zanes'd all heard these stories umpteen times. Mr. Chapman would sit for hours, just listening to the old man talk, even if he'd heard the stories a dozen times before.

"Mr. Chapman told us once he'd killed a rattlesnake. He was wading through thick brush and that rattler came out of nowhere and bit his ankle. He crushed the

174

snake's skull with a rock. Then he sat down and cried. The pain and poison must have been fierce, but that wasn't it. In all his years of wandering, he'd never killed another living creature, not even an insect. That's why he cried.

"Once he put a campfire out, just because mosquitoes were buzzing it. He didn't want them to singe their wings.

"According to my grandfather, it was I who first called him Johnny Appleseed. I don't remember that, though."

"Thank you, Mr. Zane."

🌳🌳🌳

"Your name for the record?" Judge Wexbury asked.

"Abner Meadows the second."

"And how do you know the defendant?"

"He saved my life during the War of 1812. My father's homestead was east of Fort Wayne, Indiana. It was Mr. Chapman who ran without stopping from our homestead south by southeast to warn pioneers about impending war parties. Johnny ran more than a hundred miles. We lit out for Mansfield and stayed in the blockhouse, the one just down this street."

The judge asked, "Why is this important?"

"There were hundreds of us refugees in Mansfield that winter. He saved us all. The good people here took care of us and our livestock. My family took the Refugee

Trail home next spring. All the homesteads were destroyed. Including ours. We would have all been killed."

"Thank you, Mr. Meadows."

Abner Meadows shook Johnny's hand and sat down.

Judge Wexbury shuffled papers, peered at documents. Suddenly, he looked up. "Mr. John Chapman?"

"Yes, sir?"

"What do you do with apple seeds?"

"I plant them in the wilderness so pioneers will have apples for the winter months, Your Honor."

"So you sold these apples for cash money?"

"No, sir. I've sold the nursery trees on occasion. Nine cents a tree."

"Nine cents," the judge said slowly. "For a tree that might live for two hundred years? How did you arrive at nine cents a tree?"

"Jonathan Hale, a man up in Bath Township, Summit County, offered me nine cents a tree for eight trees to plant on his homestead. That must have been . . . twenty years ago."

"What did you do with your seventy-two cents?"

"I gave it away. When folks give me money for trees, I give that coinage away to the poor. I have no use for money. I'd rather have Quarter Sections. I'd rather trade nursery trees for land."

Judge Wexbury frowned. "I don't understand you,

sir. You have no use for money? Nine cents a tree adds up in a hurry."

Johnny shrugged. "I don't have any pockets."

Johnny's friends and family chuckled. "That's our Johnny!" someone shouted.

The judge glared at them all.

"And what of your taxes, Mr. Chapman?"

Everyone leaned forward to listen. Johnny said slowly, "I've had plenty of time to think about that, Your Honor. I'm real sorry. I've paid my taxes here in Richland County, mostly so my name wouldn't appear in the newspaper and embarrass my sister. Other than that . . . I'm real sorry. Mr. Clawstraight was right—I haven't rendered therefore unto Caesar. That does mean taxes."

Just then a slight, middle-aged woman stood up. "Your Honor, might I speak? I've come all the way from Hurricane, Missouri."

"Your name?"

"Susannah Roscoe."

Who's this? I don't recognize her.

"You may," Judge Wexbury said.

She turned to Johnny, her weather-beaten face lit up in pleasure and awe.

"You don't know me, sir, but there hasn't been a day in my memory that I haven't thought of you.

"My father owned a farm on the fork of the Little Muskingum, where it empties into the Ohio. You were passing through one day and asked my father for directions. You were looking for your friends' homesteads. Late autumn it was, 1799. More than forty years ago.

"When you told him about the apple orchard you'd planted out for us, he shot at you and sicced his dog on you. I don't know who was the meaner," she said, her voice tight with bitterness, "that horrible man or his horrible dog.

"Typhoid took him two years after. It took my brothers four winters after that. It was just Ma, my little sister, Anne, and myself.

"A year later, we had apples. Those apples saved our lives. In later years, Anne and I sold apples to westering pioneers heading down the Ohio on broadhorns. They were grateful for the fruit. We were grateful for the cash.

"My husband farmed that land. For years I kept hoping to see you, to thank you. I thought surely you'd come down the Ohio again."

"That was your father?" Johnny exclaimed. "And you were one of those children, fanned out behind your mother's skirt? I did come down the Ohio, every autumn for years and years. I always avoided your farm. I was afraid. I'm sorry, Mrs. Roscoe. My fear overcame me. It betrayed us both."

"That's all right, Mr. Chapman. My son-in-law's Missouri homestead has apple trees now. The seeds came from the very orchard you planted out for us, McIntosh and Ashram's Kernel.

"I give away apples to my neighbors every October. I tell them all: 'Plant the seeds so you'll have apples to give away to your neighbors someday. Just three seeds will yield a tree—a tree will yield enough fruit for an entire winter year after year.'

"Just like the parable of the loaves and the fishes," Mrs. Roscoe said, her face shining, "apples are a blessing four-thousand-fold."

She sat down while Judge Wexbury shuffled papers. "These folks and plenty more want me to dismiss the charges against you," he said. "What say you to that, Mr. Chapman?"

Freedom!

For a long moment Johnny gazed at the circle of friends in the chairs.

There's Captain Welton! And Phineas Filo, all the way from Pittsburgh! I'd recognize Zanes anywhere, with those dark eyes and hair. And Helen Stadden. That can't be Willie Van Kirk! That can't be Molly Van Swearingen! The Claxtons, the Hessels, and the Faulkners from the Refugee Trail.

"Thank you, all of you. Thank you for your kindness, for coming all this way to help me when I needed your help the most."

Johnny turned to the judge. "God gave me my mission, Your Honor. I've been directed to walk my circle as long as I am able."

"I've been looking at your Quarter Section deeds, Mr. Chapman. You own thousands of acres."

"The orchards belong to God, your Honor. If I'm sure of one thing in this life, it's that."

Judge Wexbury shot him a look. "Are you saying you won't sell this land? You won't bequeath these acres to someone else when you die?"

"I own no land."

Judge Wexbury picked up quill and paper. He wrote in silence—the only noise was the quill's nib scratching across the page.

Finally, he pushed the sheet across his desk.

"Sign this, Mr. Chapman. Sign it, and you're a free man."

🌳🌳🌳

That afternoon, Johnny stood in front of the Mansfield prison, blinking into the brisk October sunlight. A crowd of cheering people pressed around him.

Persis shouted, "What did you sign, Johnny?"

He shouted back, "I agreed not to sell or bequeath lands in Ohio to anyone upon my death. Signed and dated."

The crowd cheered.

Johnny rubbed his hands together. "The Wisconsin Territory, sister—Danes, Swedes, and Norwegians are pouring into the lands around Fort Snelling. I'm ready to go."

"Johnny, you can't go to Fort Snelling," Persis cried. "You're an old man! Your mind is failing! You can't live among those Scandihoovians, claiming to be the Glory of Rome! They'll run you out or hang you first."

The way she yanked at his elbow put Johnny to mind of her husband, William, yanking at the prison bars.

"She's right, Johnny," William said. "I'd say your mission is over."

"But the Boston Belle—"

"Johnny," Persis said, as sharp as the autumn wind, "where are you going to find Boston Belle apple seeds around here?"

"Oh. I hadn't thought of that."

Why was he so tired all of a sudden, as though a great weight were pressing down on him? He'd had nine months of rest in prison.

Canada geese honked overhead, flying south. They looked like a wisp of smoke curling across the sky. It would be cold soon—the snow blowing hard against his face, the icy water seeping into his boots.

"In the spring I'll go back to Massachusetts for Boston Belle apple seeds. Then I'll walk to the Wisconsin Territory."

"Of course you will, Johnny," Persis said, yanking at his elbow. "Now it's time to go home."

"Picnic at our house, folks!" William shouted.

The crowd cheered.

SPEED FARM
1841

It's a remarkable thing, Johnny thought, and not for the first time, either: *Just cross this river, and it's like crossing into another country.*

This was not true of other rivers he'd crossed and recrossed in his long life. He'd grown up along the Connecticut River, and folks were the same on both banks.

The Hudson, the Susquehanna, the Monongahela, the Allegheny, the Big and Little Muskingum, the Scioto, the Cuyahoga, the Vermilion, the Black, the Wabash, the Whitewater, even the Mississippi—folks were pretty much the same from one side of the river to the other. They were neighbors.

But cross the Ohio into Kentucky, and everything was different, everything but his apple trees.

The food was different. Here, people ate rice and gravy instead of potatoes with their chicken, mustard

183

greens instead of string beans, ham instead of beef, pecan pie instead of fruit pie.

The houses were different. Here, people lived in sprawling, whitewashed homes with deep porches as protection against the sun.

The crops were different. Here, people grew cotton, tobacco, rice, and indigo instead of corn, wheat, beans, and potatoes.

The people were different as well. Here, everybody moved slower than people did north of the river. Kentuckians talked slower, walked slower, ate slower, drank slower, danced slower, courted slower, farmed slower, lived slower, probably died slower, too, Johnny thought.

They took the time to be polite with one another. It was as though the heat and the long summers made everybody and everything slow down to make up for it. It put him in mind of molasses, the whole state awash in it. Any sort of movement took real effort.

He'd never seen a manufactory in Kentucky, either. It was just too hot for ironworks and foundries, he reckoned.

Instead, he saw quiet plantations and rich pastures. At sunrise and sunset, when the shadows of the lush grass blades were just right, those green pastures glowed blue.

In those pastures were the most beautiful horses he'd ever seen. He took to leaning against fence posts for hours, just for the sheer joy of watching them and listening to them. They cropped the succulent grass and swished at flies with their long, shining tails.

The air was filled with the spicy-sweet scent of torn fodder. And the foals! All long, knobby legs and fuzzy coats, they'd peek at him from behind their mothers— their huge eyes a soft, questioning brown.

Every once in a while the horses would take off at a gallop, for no reason Johnny could fathom. They'd race through the fields—manes and tails flying, nostrils flaring, muscles rolling under glossy brown coats, hooves like distant thunder—with foals skittering after them. Then they'd stop and calmly crop the grass again.

The whole point to Kentucky is these horses. They're like royalty.

One hot summer afternoon, Johnny stopped at a plantation outside of Louisville with a sign at the gate: Speed Farm. He smiled to himself, for there was very little here he could reckon as speedy. Even the river, more a stream really, just meandered along, slow as molasses in January.

Maybe the birds were speedy, flying after insects? No—they seemed slower, too. Did that mean the insects were slower here? Was that possible?

A young man called out from beside the stream. "May I help you, sir?"

The young man was fishing, if you could call it

that—he was stretched out against a pin oak, impossibly long legs propping up a fishing pole. The line was tangled in duckweeds. Next to him were books scattered every which way.

"Good day to you," Johnny replied. He walked toward the man. The closer he got, the more astonished he became.

Why, this young man could have been himself, had Johnny been sitting by this stream thirty-five years before! How could that be?

Johnny was the first to admit his eyes weren't what they used to be: It was as though he walked through a thick fog now. The drowsy summer heat, and the young man . . . Johnny's mind drifted backward or maybe sort of sideward. He floated along in the cloudy stillness, not really sure what year it was.

This young man's thick hair was the same shade of brown Johnny's used to be. The deep-set eyes were the same clear brown. He had the same heavy eyebrows and squared-off chin. Even his body was the same—long and thin with great bulges at the elbows and knees, like knobs on a hickory tree.

"May I help you, sir?" the young man repeated.

"I was just thinking how much alike we are. We could be twins!"

The man looked Johnny over slowly. His face stretched into a wry grin.

"That's—that's not what I meant," Johnny stammered. He didn't want this young man to think he was feeble-minded. "I mean, how much I used to look like you, thirty-five years ago."

"I see," the man said. "So that means I'll look like you in thirty-five years? I reckon I could do worse."

Johnny grinned back at him. "Only if you let your hair and beard grow. I haven't cut mine since . . . I don't even remember. Since before you were born, probably."

The man arched his eyebrows. "I was thirty-two years old last February. You haven't cut your hair or beard since 1809?"

"Since 1805. They keep me warm as a blanket in the winter. Lately I've been braiding them both for the summer."

"So how long are they, your hair and beard?"

"Almost to my ankles."

The man rubbed his smooth face. "Like Samson's. Can you slay one thousand men with the jawbone of a donkey?"

Johnny laughed. "I can't say I ever tried."

"Maybe I'll let my whiskers grow someday. Just not as long as yours," said the man.

Johnny sat down next to him. "Is this your farm? Speed Farm? I'm looking for open land to plant apple seeds on."

"No, no. This farm belongs to a friend of mine,

Joshua Speed. You'll have to talk to him. He invited me down here for the summer."

"A friendly visit, then."

The young man's face darkened. "No. Convalescence. I've had my share of setbacks, Mr. Chapman. You are Johnny Appleseed, aren't you?"

Johnny nodded. He'd long since gotten used to being recognized everywhere he went.

"I know what I have to do, Mr. Chapman. I know what those first steps have to be. I just can't seem to take those first steps. I can't make any money. I can't find a woman who will marry me. I should have settled into my occupation by now. I should have gotten those first steps taken care of long since.

"My ambitions are slipping away," he said sadly. "So I've come here to watch a summer's worth of my life recede further. And to try to decide what to do about it."

"You don't sound like a Kentuckian."

"I was born here," the young man said. "I grew up in Indiana. I live across the river in Illinois now."

"I was just thinking how different it is here. Just cross the Ohio, and it's like entering into another nation."

"Sometimes I think we are in another nation, Mr. Chapman. I've been to the Deep South. I worked on a steamboat once, all the way to New Orleans, when I was eighteen. New Orleans might as well be another world entirely."

The man's hands hardened into fists. "It's our nation's curse, sir. Slavery."

"You're right," Johnny replied.

"We politicians will try to find some way out, but it's a curse," the young man continued. "A curse that will be absolved only with bloodshed, I'm afraid."

"You're a politician? I thought you were a farmer."

The young man looked shocked. "No, no, the farmer's life is not for me. Those books . . ." He pointed to the stacks crowded around his feet.

"I taught myself to read. English. Greek. Latin. The law."

"That's quite a first step," Johnny said.

The young man smiled again. "That it was, Mr. Chapman."

Johnny thought this young man had about the saddest face he'd ever seen, as though he held the world's sorrow in his eyes. And yet his whole demeanor changed when he smiled. Johnny wanted him to smile again.

"What do you do in Illinois?" he asked.

The young man's face darkened again. "What haven't I done?" he groaned. "I've been a farmhand, a soldier, a store owner, a surveyor, a boatswain, a postmaster, a lawyer, a state representative. I've failed at them all."

"Which one did you enjoy doing the most?"

"That's easy. I enjoy two of them so much, it's work

I'd gladly do for nothing if I could afford to: The law and politics."

Johnny looked away. He'd tangled with the law once in his life, and once was enough. As for politics—he hadn't given it a second thought since James Bushnell had told him about Thomas Jefferson's presidential campaign. Thomas Jefferson couldn't still be president, could he? Were such things possible?

More than half a lifetime ago.

The men were quiet for a moment, lost in thought. Johnny's companion cast his fishing line farther out into the stream. The sinker and line tangled quickly in the duckweeds again.

"It seems to me," Johnny said slowly, "that God has given you your mission. He wants you to use the law, and politics, to end slavery."

The young man stared at him in amazement.

"I say that because I've been studying your face. You seemed so angry back then, talking about New Orleans and slavery."

The young man fastened his keen gaze on Johnny. "You believe in missions." It was said as a statement, not a question. "What would you do, Johnny Appleseed? What would you do about slavery?"

"When I was your age, I would have said, 'Blessed are the meek: for they shall inherit the earth.' But now . . . I don't know." Johnny's voice fell away.

Out of the corner of his eye, he saw the young man still staring at him intently. "I do indeed believe in missions," Johnny said quickly. "There are so many problems in this world, we ought to invite as many solutions as there are people to solve them.

"I knew when I was sixteen that I'd be doing something with apples; just exactly what, I didn't know until October of 1799. I'll never forget the moment I knew. My life began to sprout, bursting from the seed. Most boys have an occupation by the time they're fourteen, fifteen. I was twenty-five years old."

"I'm thirty-two." The young man had that dark, bleak look on his face again.

"The greater the mission, the longer it takes for it to grow, for you to find it within yourself," Johnny said quickly. "Like a black walnut tree—it grows the slowest, and hence the strongest. When I was growing up, as a boy in Massachusetts, it seemed to me that a black walnut tree was just about the most glorious thing God had created."

"A black walnut tree," the young man said thoughtfully. He picked up his fishing pole. "Will you stay for dinner? I'm sure you'd be welcome."

"Oh, these days all I feel like eating is corn mush. I noticed a blackberry bramble back there a piece. I'll eat the blackberries."

The young man stood up. "I'd heard that about you.

That's something else we have in common, Mr. Chapman. I don't eat meat either." He held his fishing line up to Johnny.

There was no hook on the line. Johnny laughed. "So you weren't really fishing?"

The young man helped him to his feet. "Sometimes a person just sitting unsettles folks. A fishing pole helps. I've enjoyed talking to you, Mr. Chapman. I'll remember your advice: A black walnut tree grows the slowest, and hence is the strongest."

"You didn't tell me your name."

The young man leaned forward and shook Johnny's hand. "My name is Abraham Lincoln." He lifted his left hand and pointed a long finger toward the plantation house. "I'll be able to tell my friend that I met Johnny Appleseed today. A real honor, sir."

Johnny drifted backward again in time, or maybe forward, as though he were floating and this young man's steady grip were his only ballast. He was still rattled: In his opinion, their resemblance was uncanny. Gazing into this sad, kindly face was like peering into his own from years gone by. It was like staring into time itself.

"Sometimes I think our lives circle right around to greet us," Johnny said, "to face us and to shake our hands. We look beyond our shoulder to see where we've been."

"Is that so?"

"Mr. Lincoln, the best sort of mission is one that begets kindness. For kindness begets kindness, sir: four-thousand-fold."

"Are you sure you won't join us for dinner, Mr. Chapman? You could have a nap in a rocking chair first."

"A nap on a Kentucky plantation porch would be close to Paradise, Mr. Lincoln. I reckon I will. Thank you, sir."

Afterword

Nearly everyone in *The Sun, the Rain, and the Apple Seed* was a real person. The only fictional characters are the Van Kirks' butler, Judge Wexbury, Mr. Clawstraight, Susannah Roscoe, and the families on the Refugee Trail. The names of Isaac Stadden's children are fictional, too.

When Johnny Appleseed died on March 18, 1845, he was wearing a burlap coffee sack for a shirt, or rather a tunic. He had on one boot and one shoe, and four pairs of pants that he'd split up the inseams and overlapped around his waist like roof shingles. A rope held the pants up and also served double duty to keep his Bible in place around his middle. He had made a hole in the coffee-sack tunic to pass the rope through. He had his cornmeal sack, his saucepan, and his apple seed pouches.

Johnny Appleseed died in Fort Wayne, Indiana. He was in Fort Wayne for the spring planting of apple seeds.

His good friend William Worth found Johnny Appleseed early one morning leaning against his house. He was delirious, but according to Mr. Worth, Johnny's face was "shining with happiness."

Dr. Samuel C. Fetter attended his dying hours and said he'd never seen a patient "in so placid a state at the approach of death." Johnny died in William Worth's bed.

His grave is part of the Johnny Appleseed National Memorial Park in Fort Wayne, Indiana. His monument reads, "He lived for others."

His trees grow still. My first-grade teacher's farm park, Allardale, on Remsen Road in Medina County, Ohio, has a Johnny Appleseed tree growing in a shady spot below a ridge. Allardale is part of the Medina County Parks System.

In early May, the rural landscapes of Ohio, Indiana, southern Illinois, and Kentucky are covered in delicate apple blossoms.

John Chapman's Bible is in the Richland Historical Society in Mansfield, Ohio. The deep groove down the center of the cover was made by the rope that he used to tie the Bible around his middle. The most worn passages are the Psalms, with entire corners missing from some of the pages.

195

John Chapman lived the second half of his life during the Great Awakening, a time of sweeping religious fervor in the United States. It also marked the beginning of national compulsory public education. It was not unusual for a nineteenth-century American to read the Bible often, and to quote memorized verses to others.

Even so, John Chapman was known for his extraordinary knowledge of the Bible.

THE WAR OF 1812

General William Hull did lose Detroit, Michigan, to the British and their Shawnee allies in August of 1812. Johnny Appleseed ran for three days and nights nonstop, shouting warnings to the pioneers in northeast Indiana and northwest Ohio. I've quoted his actual words of warning. Loaded as this warning was with Biblical allusions, and considering the situation (the run itself, the life-or-death drama, the need to move quickly), I can only wonder if he talked this way all the time.

He told the pioneers to flee to Mansfield, Ohio. The blockhouse, in which people and animals hid, is still standing. A monument to Johnny Appleseed's courage is just to the right of the blockhouse.

SWEDENBORGIANS

No one knows when John Chapman became a follower of the eighteenth-century Swedish mystic Emanuel Swedenborg. Swedenborg believed that mystic prayer and meditation would usher in the New Jerusalem, a time of peace and plenty. There would be communion with the angels, and with God. Johnny Appleseed considered himself a Swedenborgian missionary to the people of the North American wilderness. He carried Swedenborg's texts with him, often breaking the books into three or four sections and lending them out to friends. He frequently preached about the New Jerusalem.

He wrote about his mission to what were certainly the astonished church elders in Sweden. His letters are in the Swedish National Museum in Stockholm.

TEXAS INDEPENDENCE

Texans declared their independence from Mexico on March 2, 1836. The Battle of the Alamo followed four days later. On April 21, 1836, Texans, aided by American soldiers, chased General Santa Anna and his men into Buffalo Bayou during the Battle of San Jacinto, a battle the Texans and Americans won. More American soldiers left for Texas that summer.

CORNPLANTER

Cornplanter, whose English name was John O'Bail, died in 1836, when he was approximately one hundred one years old. His band of Seneca left Indiana after the War of 1812. He secured land for his people along the Allegheny River in Pennsylvania, just south of the New York State border.

TAXES

John Chapman once owned approximately 1200 acres in the state of Ohio. He owned 227 acres, and one gray mare, in the state of Indiana. Indiana sold his land and his mare to cover his debts, including $3.44 for laying him out for his funeral and $6.00 for his coffin. There is nothing in his estate papers about land in Ohio.

As described in the story, John Chapman was charged for non-payment of taxes to the state of Ohio. These charges were later dropped.

John Chapman lost his acres in the state of Ohio as partial payment for more than forty years of delinquent taxes and unpaid mortgages. Libraries, courthouses, town halls, schools, hospitals, orphanages, county homes, and prisons were built on land once tilled by Johnny Appleseed.

ABRAHAM LINCOLN

Whether or not John Chapman ever met Abraham Lincoln is a matter much debated among historians and scholars. We know Johnny Appleseed was famous in the last half of his life; people sought him out. We know he planted apple seeds in Kentucky in the early 1840s. We also know that Abraham Lincoln was in Louisville, Kentucky, the summer of 1841.

Abraham Lincoln was there for an extended visit with his friend

Joshua Speed, on Speed Farm. Lincoln was invited to Speed Farm to recover from what we would now refer to as severe depression.

As a young man, Abraham Lincoln was harshly critical of people. As he got older, he appealed to "the better angels of our natures."

A Novel of a Life

Johnny Appleseed was a real person, so why is this account a novel and not a biography?

There are many biographies about Johnny Appleseed. They all, in my opinion, touch only lightly on an uncomfortable fact: John Chapman wasn't right in the head.

It was an angel who first appeared to him in Pittsburgh. This angel told him to plant apple seeds in the borderlands.

As he planted his apple seeds, an army of angels walked behind him in the wilderness. His spirit-wives were his constant companions; the three of them walked together and talked together.

As he slept under the stars, those stars became angels. Angels sang to him each and every night he spent out-of-doors. Their music was more beautiful than the bluebird's song.

These angels, these messengers from God, were as real to him as his own family and friends.

What are we to make of his visions and the voices he heard in his head? Johnny Appleseed was surely as confounding and perplexing a person in the nineteenth century as he is in the twenty-first century.

I believe we may better understand Johnny Appleseed if we get closer to his visions and voices. A novel can evoke the fanciful and fantastic in a way that a biography cannot.

Johnny Appleseed was a man who lived generations ahead of his time. He was an abolitionist, a pacifist, a conservationist, and a vegetarian. He treated everyone equally, with respect and kindness.

We can no longer "save the seeds for Johnny Appleseed," but we can best remember him and honor his work by planting trees. We can also learn from his example and treat one another with the same respect and kindness.

Sources

Biblical quotations are from the Holy Bible, the King James Version, The New Open Bible Study Edition, Thomas Nelson, Inc., Nashville, Tenn., 1990.

Quotations and allusions are from the following books: Genesis, Exodus, Judges, Psalms, Ecclesiastes, Isaiah, Jeremiah, Lamentations, Hosea, Joel, Amos, Matthew, Luke, John, I and II Corinthians, Hebrews.

Bath Historical Society, Old Town Hall, Bath, Ohio, 44210.

Bierce, Lucius V. *Historical Reminiscences of Summit County.* Akron, Ohio: T. & H. G. Canfield, Publishers, 1854.

Birlingame, Michael. *The Inner World of Abraham Lincoln.* Urbana, Ill.: University of Illinois Press, 1994.

Dalai Lama XIV and Howard C. Cutler, M.D. *The Art of Happiness: A Handbook for Living.* New York: Riverhead Books, 1998.

DeYoung, Laura. "Facilities and Natural Resource Inventory and GIS Mapping, Mohican-Malabar Regional Master Plan, Map 11: Archaeological and Historical Sites in Study Area." Kent, Ohio: Davey Resource Group, 1999.

Dirlam, H. Kenneth. *John Chapman, "by Occupation a Gatherer and Planter of Appleseeds."* Mansfield, Ohio: the Richland County Historical Society, 1954.

Donald, David Herbert. *Lincoln.* New York: Simon & Schuster, 1995.

Haferd, Laura. "Richfield on Search for Forgotten Fruit—Historians Hope to Find Lost Apple Trees of Captain Elijah Welton." *Akron Beacon Journal,* October 16, 2000.

Haley, William D. "Johnny Appleseed—A Pioneer Hero." In *Harper's New Monthly Magazine,* November 1871, pp. 830–36.

Haudenosaunee Homework Help Team at the website: www.peace4turtleisland.org

Jones, William Ellery. *New Information About an Old Friend.* West Chester, Pa.: The Swedenborg Press, 1945, reprinted 1998. Founder and president of the Johnny Appleseed Heritage Center, Mansfield, Ohio.

Leonard, John William. *Pittsburgh and Allegheny Illustrated Review: Historical, Biographical, and Commercial. A Record of Progress in Commerce, Manufactures, the Professions, and in Social and Municipal Life.* Pittsburgh, Pa: J. M. Elstner, 1889.

Marshall, Leslie, ed. *Johnny Appleseed, a Voice in the Wilderness: The Story of the Pioneer John Chapman.* Paterson, N.J.: The Swedenborg Press, 1945. Reprinted West Chester, Pa.: Chrysalis Books, 2000.

The Ohio Historical Society, 1982 Velma Ave., Columbus, Ohio. *The Estate of John Chapman, 1845.*

Okey, Robin. *The Habsburg Monarchy: From Enlightenment to Eclipse.* New York: St. Martin's Press, 2001.

Perkins, Bradford. *The Causes of the War of 1812: National Honor or National Interest?* New York: Holt, Rinehart and Winston, 1962.

Smith, Ophia D. "The Story of Johnny Appleseed." In Marshall, Leslie, ed. *Johnny Appleseed, a Voice in the Wilderness: The Story of the Pioneer John Chapman.* Paterson, N.J.: The Swedenborg Press, 1945. Reprinted West Chester, Pa.: Chrysalis Books, 2000.